THE
RESTING SPOT

SCOTT HENDRIX

"To die, to sleep; To sleep, perchance to dream: Ay, there's the rub; For in that sleep of death what dreams may come."

Hamlet by William Shakespeare

Night

F lashes. *Just flashes. Each time he closed his eyes there were flashes. Flashes of his father. Only his father. Of all the people he knew in his life, of all of the people he saw every day, the only face he ever saw in dreams was his father's.*

When night fell, he knew the flashes would flood the dark. He delayed crawling into bed and always fought sleep until the heaviness of the day fell upon him, forcing it.

There was never any order to them, the dreams. Different images from his childhood appeared in randomness; they lay constant on his mind, heaviness that only an unrepentant mind knows.

A gray shadowy figure standing sparse of reality, frail and drunk, sneering, flashed. The figure doesn't speak, but is heard. Words given to memory push to the forefront in the dark.

A figure walking on a long green fairway, flush with drink, steel faced, flashed. Again, nothing heard, but rather memory of random vestiges of words stung like barbed wire wrapping around an ear, squeezing and tightening, flashed.

Then the figure lays dormant staring at a hovering site above him. A thud sounding, splaying the right-side temple and fixing his gaze that ended his life ... that spirit forever leaving the earth, its remains covered by soil until it's washed away revealing all that is left.

Morning arrives, dark dispenses into light, and the flashes end. The dream is over until evening, the secret lives every day.

CHAPTER ONE

Hugh Jack Rives was a disgraced, pill popping, whisky swigging attorney on his fourth marriage. He carried a gun for protection, mainly from jealous husbands and a myriad of disgruntled clients that he had wronged over the years.

His name usually provoked a mixed bag of emotions. He could easily be loved and hated at the same time and by the same person. Under suspicion and investigated by the State Bar for a litany of offenses, he was recently stripped of his ability to legally practice law in the State of Mississippi.

Corrupt as any man could be, both ethically and morally, Hugh Jack seemed unable or unwilling to differentiate between knowing the Bible cover to cover, and creating elaborate illegal schemes to sue insurance companies.

Injury law was Hugh Jack's life. For his entire career he had been unscrupulous, breaking most of the laws he was meant to uphold. He consistently loaned money to clients prior to receiving their settlement and charged them ridiculous amounts of interest. He had a habit of prolonging the process to continue earning the interest, and by the time the client's settlement check was cut, he had taken the majority of it.

The illegal loans, interest payments, and the pills to reduce stress finally caught up with him. He served no jail time. Instead of going to prison, he wrangled a slap on the wrist and detoxed in a drug rehabilitation center. From there he went to south Mississippi for sex addiction counseling. He threw that in the mix to make his case for rehabilitation more appealing, an olive branch of sorts. Fifty thousand dollars to the right judge, and like magic, no prison time and a hospital stay where he was forced to talk about sex all day.

He had just completed his final legal negotiation, on the final case of his career, with the Farmer's Best Insurance Company and their trove of attorneys, all young and too buttoned up for his liking. They all looked like they just arrived at a fraternity meeting, spit shined, combed, and pressed. To Hugh Jack, they simply looked too honest to deal with, which made his job tougher.

Regardless of their age and appearance, they were tough negotiators, but not tough enough. Hugh Jack got what he wanted.

The young attorneys didn't know as much about the case as they thought. They didn't know that Hugh Jack's clients had well below average intelligence. His two main clients, beneficiaries of their father's suit, would only be paid fifty thousand dollars each from the one million dollar settlement. They didn't know the post office box where they would send the check was obtained by Hugh Jack himself; and they didn't know the name they were printing on the check, Knox Inc., was a shell company created to funnel Hugh Jack's money. They also didn't know the list of names Hugh Jack provided as possible future litigants in a class action lawsuit were fake. The people were real; their stories were not.

The one thousand dollars Hugh Jack paid them individually to use their names was a good investment. Through the attorneys, the company quietly paid an extra million cash under the table to keep their names off of any future lawsuit and the issue out of the press. They had no idea the majority of the money would go directly into Hugh Jack's pocket. He profited ninety-nine thousand per person. A stroke of genius on his part he thought.

The two surviving sons of Bud McCowan, now under the impression they were simply part of a class action lawsuit, would get fifty thousand each, more money than they had ever seen.

The lawsuit was their father's, and after he died, they were just happy to get anything at all. They had never known about the case, didn't care about the case, and didn't really have the mental capacity to understand the legalities of it anyway. They wanted enough money to party and chase women for as long as the money lasted. Then they would go back to living on their disability checks, along with the money from their remarried wealthy mother.

Bud McCowan discovered the secret the company didn't want exposed, and he eventually died from it. He was so fearful of retribution by the company that he only told Hugh Jack on his death bed minutes before he died. He told him everything, and as any good attorney would, Hugh Jack used that information in his negotiations.

High from his win, Hugh Jack sped north on Highway Forty-nine, headed to Goldie's, one of the last remaining houses of ill repute on the coast. He had already called ahead, Kat would be waiting. He planned to spend two days in her company, drink bourbon, and put a huge dent in a box of Don Tomas cigars.

His hands kept rhythm on the steering wheel as Creedence Clearwater Revival's "Suzie Q" played. When the car in front of him began weaving wildly, he slowed, allowing several car lengths to develop between them.

During his waking moments, Hugh Jack thought of two things, injury law and women. He pulled over, watching and imagining the eminent wreck. His mind running through a list of attorneys he could send the case to and work out some sort of agreement between the two of them.

He was ready to jump out and drop off a few business cards to the injured and hoped someone else called for help. He pulled a business card from his brief case and stared at it, "Hell, I can't use these anymore," Hugh Jack said out loud and threw the card in his floorboard.

As he watched and waited, the car finally spun off the highway onto the shoulder and down into the ditch, kicking up rocks and thick mud. The car finally rose out of the ditch and violently rocked back and forth, as if someone prematurely threw it in park, before it was able to come to a complete stop.

The car still rocked when a petite blonde wearing daisy dukes and a white Guns and Roses t-shirt tied above her navel jumped out, stumbling in the loose rocks. She opened the back door and grabbed a small duffle bag and baseball bat. Throwing the duffle bag on the ground, she swung the bat and hit the windshield, finally shattering it on the fourth swing. She busted both headlights, and on her way toward the driver, she flattened his side-view mirror. She stuck the end of the bat through the window, poking as hard as she could, eventually landing a few licks on the driver's face.

Finally, having enough, she threw down the bat, picked up her duffle bag, and started walking, turning and cursing the occupant with each step.

"Crazy old bastard, pervert piece of shit!" she screamed as she turned slightly and flipped him the bird.

"Damn, look at that little honey go," Hugh Jack said out loud to himself, smiling, injecting the fat butt of a cigar between his teeth.

He shifted the Mercedes in drive and pulled up beside her. "Hey little Darlin', you need a ride?"

"Leave me the hell alone," the girl said, as tears rolled down her face and she gasped for a breath.

The Mercedes continued along beside her as sirens filled the still, muggy afternoon air. "Cops are comin'. You better come on," Hugh Jack hollered through his window.

The girl looked around her, heard the sirens, and quickly jumped into the back seat and screamed, "Go!"

"Hugh Jack Rives, Attorney at Law," he said, sticking his thick hand as far behind him as his heft would allow. The greeting went unmet.

The girl peeked out of the back glass, crouched, watching for the police.

"What's your name, Darlin'?" Hugh Jack asked staring at the abundant cleavage in his rearview mirror.

"What the hell do you care?"

"Just trying to be nice to the girl I just saved," Hugh Jack said proudly, smiling, the entire top row of his straight white teeth shining.

"Hell, I didn't see you nowhere when I was beatin' that man's ass with his own bat. Where the hell were you?"

"You're not sittin' in jail right now, are you?" Hugh Jack asked. "What's your name?"

"Nickie ... my damn name's Nickie. You satisfied?"

"What was all that about back there?"

"You're a nosy bastard ain't you? You cowboy lookin' son of a bitch."

"Just concerned about you, Darlin.'"

"Just another damn pervert. I can't even just get a ride nowhere without a man trying to have me," Nickie said, letting out a frustrated growl.

"Well, it doesn't help with the way you're dressed, Darlin'. How old are you?"

"Twenty-two damn years old. How old are you old man?"

"Old enough to be your granddaddy," Hugh Jack said, suddenly aging himself back to his sixty-four years.

"Where you headin'?" Hugh Jack asked peering at her in the rearview.

"I ain't really got nowhere to be," Nickie said, as if she had answered that question before. "What kind of a redneck country ass name is Hugh Jack anyway?"

"That's the name my daddy gave me, same as his and my granddaddy's. I'm the third."

Nickie sat in the backseat with her hand in her bag holding an opened pocket knife in a tight grip, ready should "granddaddy" try to make a move on her.

She watched Hugh Jack as he opened his modified glove compartment scanning the humidor for a good smoke. He hesitated, exchanging glances with the road and the selection of cigars in front of him. He finally picked an Arturo Fuente and put it to his nose. He moved the length along his upper lip, inhaling as he did.

The cigar completed Hugh Jack Rives. His cowboy hats

were formed in Texas in the same small town where his boots were custom made from exotic leathers. On his right hand he wore the largest class ring available from 1956, the year he graduated from Mississippi State. On his left, he wore the largest one Ole Miss had four years later when he received his Juris Doctor degree.

He drove a silver green metallic S Class Mercedes. The S class allowed enough head room for his hat to remain atop his head, which was a big selling point. He only took his hat off when he stepped indoors or met a lady.

Hugh Jack was a product of a childhood soaked in gentility. He was raised to be a gentleman by a Southern belle mother and a self-made father made wealthy by oil and timber.

"You gonna light that thang?" Nickie asked, watching Hugh Jack like a hawk.

"Plannin' on it Darlin'," Hugh Jack said as he cut the end and then stuck the butt in his mouth, wetting it.

"You gon' smoke me out back here."

"Well, why don't you just move on up here," Hugh Jack said, smiling at Nickie as he lit the cigar, twisting it in his mouth, and watching as the back seat filled with smoke. Nickie waved it away from her nose, frowning.

"Naw, you just trying to get me up there with you. Then you gon' try to feel me up or something."

"I won't, but suit yourself," Hugh Jack said, taking three large puffs and blowing the smoke toward the roof, watching as the air conditioner assisted filling the backseat.

"So where are you from?" Hugh Jack questioned as he twisted the diamond horseshoe ring on his fat little finger, straightening it.

"I guess you could say I'm from the coast, but I've lived

all over … damn pull over," Nickie yelled, coughing and fanning the smoke.

Still coughing, she climbed into the large front seat. Sitting next to Hugh Jack, she felt weak and vulnerable. He could overpower her, be on top and have his way with her in seconds.

"You see this. Try anything and it'll be inside you before you can blink," she said, brandishing the knife, waving it around to make her point. "Crack your damn winda."

Hugh Jack pulled into a driveway that led to a large, white antebellum home located just off of the beach.

"I need to run in here for just a few minutes. I'll be right back."

"This where you live?" Nickie asked, as she nervously sat straighter in the seat.

"Nope, just need to take care of some business real quick. Be right back," Hugh Jack said, plopping his cigar into his smiling mouth.

He stepped quickly through the front door, removed his hat, and smoothed his hair back, while women swarmed to his side. Hugh Jack disappeared as the front door closed.

Nickie had fallen asleep with her head against the window when she was awakened by a tapping near her ear. An older blonde woman in a flowing silk gown and a long feather boa stood outside the car. She rolled the window down just as Hugh Jack walked out of the front door, adjusting his large turquoise belt buckle so it was straight and lined up with his fly.

He walked over to the woman and kissed her on the lips.

"Thank you, Goldie. Sorry I had to cut things short Darlin, I'll see y'all soon."

"She's cute," Goldie said, staring at Nickie. "How old are you honey?"

"Twenty-two."

"Sure is young, Hugh."

"Why do you think I'm here," Hugh Jack said as he grabbed another cigar, cut it, lit it, and put the car in reverse.

"Ok Darlin, where am I takin' you?"

"I don't know, do you know about any cheap motels close by?" Nickie asked.

"I know where a very cheap one is in Lewiston, where I'm from."

"Look, I ain't shackin' up with you, so just get that out of your head."

"Listen, I have a little apartment in my barn. It's near a golf course, it's very nice, you're welcome to stay there for a while if you need to."

"Do you live there?" Nickie asked.

"Not unless you want me too," Hugh Jack said, winking at Nickie.

"I don't, if that's how you expect me to pay you back, I'll just move on."

"You don't have to pay me a thing."

"Okay, but I'll cut you, if you try anything."

Hugh Jack smiled at Nickie, stuck his cigar in his mouth, and pointed the car north and started back home toward Lewiston.

CHAPTER TWO

Rain poured for three weeks straight. The rivers and creeks had risen to dangerously high levels, flooding the lower roads now only used by fish and turtles and things that swam.

It was early September; hurricane season wouldn't end for another three months. Hurricane Alice had been busy bouncing all over the Atlantic for nearly two weeks dumping tons of water along the eastern seaboard, eventually working its way toward the Gulf of Mexico. Now, the wind along with the rain had blown inland two hundred plus miles to the north.

Travel proved to be impossible for smaller cars, while trucks with large tires and four-wheel drive provided the only safe mode of transportation. In the midst of the flooding and the rain Hugh Jack drove. He drove around Lewiston aimlessly... avoiding. Avoiding mistresses. Avoiding the clients he had wronged. Avoiding his new wife. Avoiding the realization his life had taken such a terrible turn. He spent his days avoiding what his life had become.

Nickie had been living in the barn's loft apartment since he picked her up from the side of the highway. The original plan of a few days had turned into two and a half weeks. So far, she wasn't budging; and so far, wife number four hadn't found out about her. He accepted that she was getting more comfortable being there, and he had yet to strike up a romance with her.

The possibility plagued his mind daily, but for some strange reason had not yet made the move. He worried that he was losing his touch, getting too old. But there was something about Nickie that just didn't allow those thoughts to last too long.

In his younger days, he would have already had her in the bed and on the payroll, but there was something about this girl he just couldn't put his finger on. It might have been her looks; she was just so young. As many around Lewiston knew, it wouldn't have been the first time he had dated a girl in her twenties.

Having her at the barn was a risk. Luckily for Hugh Jack the harsh wind and rain and flooding had kept his wife and mistresses away. The irritation of the constant rain had been a blessing as well.

As he drove south from town toward the barn, the highway was all but empty. A few SUVs were slowly making their way through the flood waters careful to remain on the road and not veer off into the ditch.

As he passed Fants Grocery, a Lincoln Town Car slowly pulled out onto the highway behind him. He spotted the car in his rear view as it was closing in on him. The misty overcast day and headlights shining from the Lincoln, obscured his view of the driver. Hugh Jack sped up as their bumpers came close to touching.

"Who in the hell is this jackleg?" He asked himself out loud. "This stupid bastard's going to cause a wreck."

The Lincoln continued riding the bumper of Hugh Jack's truck. Speeding up and slowing down and weaving in and out of lanes. It hydroplaned on the puddled surface, floating across the double lines into the opposite lane before it hit a drier patch of pavement and corrected. The car could have passed Hugh Jack at any time never taking the opportunity. He sped up, trying to created distance between them. The Lincoln slowed, as it pushed into a low spot that held too much water for the heavy car.

Hugh Jack popped his cigar in his mouth and reached across the seat and opened his glove box and extracted a .45 revolver and shook the holster loose. He popped open the chamber to be sure the gun was loaded and flipped it shut. He held it, propped against the steering wheel, as he slowed and turned into his property. He stopped to switch to four-wheel drive and just as he was about to start toward the barn he was hit from behind. The Lincoln sideswiped his bumper veering into the ditch. The tank of a car sinking in the mud.

Hugh Jack pulled forward and away from the car and threw his truck in park and quickly slid from the driver's seat. He plopped onto the ground. Mud dancing up all around him. With the .45 in his hand, he kept himself braced along the side of his truck as he made his way toward the end of the bed. He crouched against the bed of his truck, taking cover, keeping the truck between him and the Lincoln. As the door to the Lincoln opened, he braced himself. A woman with wild hair and a bottle of Jack Daniels in her hand sat inside crying and cursing and beating on the steering wheel. She turned and swung her leg out of the Lincoln and sunk into the thick mud. She forced her weight out of the driver's seat and onto her feet only to slip and fall.

"Hugh Jack Rives, you're going to hell! You're nothing but a womanizing liar! Where is she?" The woman demanded, sobs following the question.

Hugh Jack still sat crouched behind his truck, leaning against his back tire, waiting for shots to ring out. The woman's voice was familiar and he slowly stood and turned toward her. He peered over the truck bed and saw a woman covered in mud and crying. He watched as she took a drink from the bottle and wiped her mouth. The bottle was half empty.

"Dammit, it's Clarice," Hugh Jack said as he relaxed and let out a breath. He slid the .45 into the waist of his pants and walked toward her.

"You said there wouldn't be anymore, then I find out you've got another mistress and now you've moved some hot little piece of young ass out here. You're such a liar!" Clarice said as he continued walking toward her.

"What's going on?" A soft voice hollered from behind Hugh Jack. Nickie stood in the doorway wearing only a tattered maroon football jersey from Hugh Jack's high school days.

"Nothin' Darlin, go on back inside I'll be in there in a minute."

"Yeah! He'll be in in a little while to service you, you little slut!" Clarice slurred among sobs. She wiped at her face again and smeared her makeup a second time. Lipstick ran at a slant from the corner of her mouth.

Hugh Jack walked over to Clarice and reached for her elbow.

"Don't you touch me," Clarice said as she jerked away from Hugh Jack with much more effort than was necessary and fell back onto the muddy ground. She sat there sobbing and took another drink from her bottle. Her slip fell below her skirt and she reached down and pulled it off of her and threw it toward Hugh Jack.

He bent down again to help her to her feet and she let him this time. He walked her into the barn. The dogs all barking and jumping as the door opened. Nickie stood above them leaning on the rail as Hugh Jack brought her in and sat her in a lawn chair.

She tucked a stray piece of hair back around her ear and took another drink and wiped mud from her hand. Hugh Jack took the whisky from her and gave her a towel to clean herself.

"Stay right here. I'm going to go get your car unstuck and then we're going to get you home," Hugh Jack said as he watched Clarice start to fade. Her eyes began to slowly flutter and she began to lean in the chair. She mumbled something as Hugh Jack walked outside.

He grabbed a chain from the bed of his truck and walked to Clarice's car and lay in the soft wet soupy mud and hooked the chain around the frame of the Lincoln. He moved his truck behind the car, hooked up the chain and pulled it out of the ditch. He pulled it out on the empty road as close to the side as he could. He moved his truck back toward the barn and walked back to the Lincoln and drove it up to the barn and parked it beside his truck.

When he stepped inside, Clarice was lying on the floor asleep. Jealous rage had changed her appearance from a beauty queen to a whisky-soaked wild woman covered in mud and smeared makeup.

"Nickie," Hugh Jack hollered.

Nickie appeared at the top of the stairs still wearing Hugh Jacks jersey.

"Can you drive?"

"Yeah."

"How about changing and come on down, I need some help getting her home," Hugh Jack said as he watched Nickie turn and go back inside the apartment.

She joined them both downstairs and she and Hugh Jack grabbed an arm and helped Clarice up and walked her out to her car.

"You drive my truck and I'll drive her home. You just follow us."

Hugh Jack and Nickie deposited Clarice at home and returned to the barn.

Buckshot Roberts Last Stand
By
Doug Hensley
Table Of Contents

Author's Notes

In the lawless frontier town of Deadwood, a lone gunslinger known only as Buckshot Roberts stands as the last line of defense between justice and chaos. When the notorious outlaw McCreedy and his brutal gang target Deadwood for conquest, only Buckshot has the skill and grit to rally the terrified townspeople against the coming storm.

Facing down McCreedy in a final showdown, Buckshot narrowly prevails but pays a high price. As he struggles back from the brink, nursing his wounds with help from the lovely Violet, news arrives that McCreedy has escaped and plans revenge with an even larger gang. Buckshot realizes their past quarrels were only the beginning - soon both sides will meet their destinies in a battle to decide Deadwood's fate once and for all.

With Violet and the residents of Deadwood looking to him for salvation, Buckshot painstakingly prepares for McCreedy's arrival. The very soul of the town hangs in the balance. When at last the day of reckoning comes, Buckshot must call upon every ounce of courage and conviction to stand against the vicious onslaught before all is lost. His greatest challenge will be embracing the light while staring into the abyss.

Chapter 1 - Buckshot Roberts Rides Into Town

The hot midday sun beat down on the dusty trail as the lone rider approached the small town of Deadwood. Though the brim of his worn leather hat was pulled down low, hints of his weathered face were visible. The man's name was Buckshot

Roberts, and his reputation as a quick-draw gunslinger preceded him wherever he went.

As Buckshot Roberts rode down the main street of Deadwood, the residents stopped to stare. Some quickly moved indoors, while others watched from the wooden sidewalks. Whispers followed in his wake, as townsfolk recognized the infamous gunman. Buckshot kept his head low and his hand rested casually on the Colt revolver strapped to his hip.

After tying up his horse at the hitching post outside the saloon, Buckshot stepped up onto the creaking boards of the porch. Taking a deep breath, he pushed through the swinging doors into the dim interior. The raucous noise inside immediately died down to a tense silence. All eyes turned cautiously toward the newcomer standing in the entrance.

"Whiskey," Buckshot growled in a low gravelly voice to the nervous bartender. The man nodded quickly and poured out a glass of their cheapest rotgut. Buckshot took his drink to a table in the far corner, keeping his back to the wall so he could see the entire room. He could feel the tension in the air like electricity.

It wasn't long before a drunk and foolish young gunslinger caught wind of the infamous Buckshot Roberts's presence. Smelling a chance to make a name for himself, the overconfident youth strode across the room to stand before Buckshot's table. "I hear tell you're one of them fast draw banditos," he declared arrogantly. "But I bet you ain't so fast against me."

A cold smile crossed Buckshot's weathered face as he slowly stood up to face the loudmouth challenger. The menacing look in the older gunman's eyes made the young man hesitate for just a second. That was all Buckshot needed. In the span of a heartbeat, he drew his shining Colt and fired a single shot that sent the kid's pistol flying from his hand.

Clutching his stinging hand, the humiliated young gunslinger quickly made for the exit. Chuckling under his breath, Buckshot twirled his revolver before sliding it smoothly back into its holster. He had made his point. Best not to push his luck any further tonight. Tossing some coins on the table, he stalked from the saloon and headed towards the small hotel across the street.

Upstairs in his rented room, Buckshot cleaned his Colt carefully and then loaded fresh bullets into the cylinder. He always made sure he was prepared. Once satisfied with his firearm, Buckshot removed his hat and boots and lay down to rest. But sleep did not find him easily...

In his dreams, Buckshot found himself back in a dusty street facing a dozen armed lawmen with guns drawn. He heard a sheriff yell, "It's over Buckshot! Throw down your weapon and surrender!" Buckshot stood defiantly, staring down the posse with fire in his eyes. "You'll never take me alive!" he shouted back. Then the deafening crack of multiple gunshots filled the air...

Buckshot awoke with a violent start, his heart racing and brow covered in sweat. It took him a moment to remember he was no longer the hunted outlaw of his past. Shaking his head bitterly, he rose and walked to the window. The moon cast an eerie glow across the silent street below. The ghosts of his past were always lurking, waiting to torment him.

At dawn, Buckshot headed downstairs where he paid for coffee and biscuits from the hotel kitchen. He ate quickly, then stepped outside onto the empty street. The sun was just peeking over the horizon, promising another scorching day ahead.

As the residents of Deadwood began to emerge sleepily from their homes, Buckshot decided to take a walk to the other end of town.

Passing by the sheriff's office, Buckshot noticed with amusement that the sheriff ducked inside and shut the door when he saw the gunslinger approaching. Clearly his reputation had preceded him. Buckshot made sure to wave friendly-like at the cowering lawman.

As the morning wore on, the streets filled with townsfolk hurrying about their business. More than a few stared suspiciously at the unfamiliar figure among them. Buckshot ignored them, but kept his eyes and ears open. He began to feel there was something unusual about the mood of this town.

It wasn't until Buckshot reached the far end of Main Street that he began to understand. A large gang of rough, dangerous-looking men were loitering outside the bank. From their horses and clothing, it was clear they were cowboys. But not just any cowboys--these men wore the distinctive bandana of the Circle K ranch. Buckshot was now on the turf of the McCreedy gang.

Jim McCreedy was the ruthless head of the Circle K. His men had a reputation for bullying and terrorizing towns all over the territory. Thieves, killers, and outlaws... McCreedy sheltered them all at his ranch in exchange for a cut of their take. Anyone who stood up to the Circle K wound up face down in a ditch. Even the lawmen were too afraid to intervene.

As Buckshot stood warily observing the gang of cowboys, the doors to the bank swung open. McCreedy himself emerged with two large sacks of cash slung over his back. The burly gang leader carried his loot towards the horses, shouting orders to his men.

Buckshot's eyes narrowed as he watched them prepare to ride out. It was clear the bank had just been robbed. These cowboys were used to getting away with anything they pleased in this town. But perhaps not today...

As the gang mounted up to leave, Buckshot strode purposefully into the street, directly in their path. His stern gaze never left McCreedy. "That money doesn't belong to you," Buckshot stated calmly but firmly.

The gang all turned towards this solitary figure standing in defiance of them. McCreedy glared down from his horse with fury and disbelief. "Out of the way, stranger," he growled through gritted teeth. "Unless you got a hankering to die today."

Buckshot didn't flinch or back down an inch. "No, I believe it is you who should be moving along," he replied, his voice steady. "Riding away and never coming back to this town." His hands hung casually near the pair of Colt pistols holstered at his hips.

For several tense seconds, the two men stared each other down in the dusty street, neither budging. The rest of the McCreedy gang watched the standoff uneasily, gripping their reins tight, ready to draw weapons if given the command. The murmuring townsfolk gathering to watch held their collective breath. They knew a storm was brewing that would soon break over Deadwood in violent fury...

Chapter 2 - Trouble Brews at the Saloon

After the tense standoff, McCreedy and his gang backed down and rode out of Deadwood, though Buckshot suspected it was not the last he'd see of them. Once the outlaws were gone, the townsfolk surged into the street, surrounding Buckshot and slapping him on the back. They were grateful someone had finally stood up to the Circle K gang, though they worried about retaliation.

Buckshot accepted their thanks politely, but made his way out of the crush of people as quick as he could. He disliked attention. As the residents of Deadwood returned to their daily business, Buckshot decided he'd earned himself a drink. He headed for the saloon once more.

Pushing through the doors into the dim interior, Buckshot found the mood inside considerably lighter than the night before. Word of his defiance of McCreedy had already spread and he was regarded warmly by the other patrons.

"Drinks are on me today for the man who drove off them Circle K hooligans!" declared the bartender jovially. He poured out whiskey for Buckshot and the handful of other customers present. Buckshot found a table in the back corner and nursed his whiskey, avoiding conversation.

Over the next hour the saloon filled up. More drinks were poured. The piano player banged out an upbeat tune. Working girls in bright dresses made their entrance, to the delight of the male clientele. The atmosphere grew increasingly lively and raucous.

Above the growing din, the saloon doors suddenly banged open violently. Falling quiet, the crowd turned to see three grim-faced men stride in. Cowboys, from their dress. And not just any cowboys--they wore the colors of the Circle K. Trouble had arrived in Deadwood.

"We're looking for a yellow-bellied snake called Buckshot Roberts," snarled the leader of the cowboys. "Word is he likes to pop off in this establishment."

From his hidden vantage, Buckshot watched the newcomers warily. Their hands rested on holstered pistols. These cowpokes were itching for a fight.

When nobody answered, the lead cowboy slammed his fist down on the bar. "I ain't asking polite," he growled. "Where's this so-called gunslinger hiding at?"

Buckshot considered his options. He didn't want to start a reckless gun battle that could get innocents killed. But perhaps these fools could be sent packing without bloodshed. Rising slowly from his seat, he stepped forward into the light.

"You called?" Buckshot said in a calm but steely voice. All eyes turned toward him.

The lead cowboy glared at him coldly. "You got some nerve showing your face after what you pulled today," he sneered. "We're here to teach you a lesson, bandit." Both men stood tensed and ready, their hands hovering close to their holstered pistols.

Looking the cowboy straight in the eyes, Buckshot spoke quietly but with absolute authority. "You picked the wrong fight. This is your last chance to walk away."

With a yell of rage, the lead cowboy went for his weapon. In a blur of motion, Buckshot's Colt was in his hand and firing. The cowboy's gun spun from his grasp as he grabbed his bloody hand and howled in pain.

His friends went for their own pistols, but Buckshot had his smoking Colt leveled at them in an instant. "Don't try it, boys," he warned. Eyes wide, they glanced at their leader and raised their hands slowly.

Keeping his gaze fixed warily on the cowboys, Buckshot spoke to the bartender. "I'd appreciate it kindly if you showed these gentlemen out." The bartender nervously came out from behind the bar and ushered the cowboys toward the door.

"McCreedy will hear about this!" the lead cowboy spat as he clutched his injured hand. "He'll burn this whole town down around you!" Then they were gone.

An uneasy silence filled the saloon. Buckshot knew there would be consequences for humiliating these Circle K men. He'd hoped to avoid further trouble, but it seemed he'd have to face McCreedy again sooner than later.

Things quieted down after the incident, though a sense of unease hung over the saloon. Buckshot kept to himself, lost in his thoughts. The arrival of a traveling preacher caught his attention. Dressed in a threadbare suit, the elderly man made his way unsteadily to the bar.

"One glass of your purest water, barkeep," the preacher requested politely. The bartender obliged, plopping a murky glass of water on the counter.

As the old man lifted it to drink, a rowdy cowboy called out mockingly. "Hey grandpa, ain't you gonna say grace before partaking of the devil's brew?" His friends chuckled stupidly.

The preacher turned towards them. "My son, though you mock me, I harbor no resentment," he said in a reedy but gentle voice. "When we leave anger and hatred behind, only then will this world know peace."

The cowboys just laughed louder. "Listen to the holy roller, will ya!" one guffawed. The preacher simply gave a sad smile and returned quietly to his drink. Buckshot felt his heart stirred by the old man's humble dignity.

Later, as the preacher left the saloon, Buckshot followed him out. He approached the elderly man outside in the street. "That was a brave thing you did back there, facing down them hooligans," he said admiringly.

The preacher waved a hand. "It is only through love that we overcome hatred." He studied Buckshot for a moment. "You seem deeply troubled, my son. If you seek peace of the soul, faith can provide it."

Buckshot looked away, unwilling to meet the old man's earnest gaze. "Some men are beyond salvation," he said bitterly. He turned and strode away down the street, leaving the preacher staring sadly after him.

As dusk fell over Deadwood, Buckshot found himself back at the saloon. It was busy again tonight, with another rowdy crowd. Buckshot sat observing the revelers pensively, wondering which among them might kill or be killed on the morrow. It seemed senseless to him.

On the far side of the room, Buckshot noticed a young woman seated alone at a table, sipping gingerly at a glass of whiskey. He was struck by her beauty--raven hair framed delicate features and vivid green eyes. But there was a profound sadness about her. What was her story?

Three drunken cowboys took notice of the lone young woman. They sauntered over to surround her table, hooting and jeering. "What's a pretty little flower like you doing in a place like this?" one leered, leaning in close. The young woman turned away, recoiling from his rancid breath.

"Come on now, darlin', don't be shy," said another cowboy, shoving his face toward her. "We just aim to show you some real Western hospitality!" They all cackled stupidly. The young woman looked around desperately, but everyone else in the saloon studiously avoided her gaze.

Having seen enough, Buckshot stood up. He approached the table and stepped between the leering cowboys and the frightened young woman. "I believe the lady would prefer to be left alone," Buckshot stated in an even but commanding voice.

The cowboys scowled at the interruption. "This ain't your concern," said the one who had first approached the woman. "We're just havin' some harmless fun." His hand drifted toward the pistol at his hip.

Buckshot stood his ground unflinchingly. "There'll be no entertainment at this woman's expense," he said. "Not while I'm here." He rested his hand casually on his own hip near his gun.

The cowboys exchanged uncertain glances, sensing his deadly seriousness. Finally the leader motioned for his friends to follow and they sulked away, grumbling under their breath.

Buckshot watched them go, then turned back to the young woman. "My apologies for the unpleasantness, miss," he said respectfully, tipping his hat. "Some men don't understand the word no."

The young woman regarded him with an expression of surprise and gratitude. "That was very kind of you, sir," she said in a soft voice. "I'm unaccustomed to anyone coming to my aid."

"Pardon my boldness, but a young lady ought not sit alone in such rough company," Buckshot said. "May I offer my protection for the remainder of your time here?"

The woman considered for a moment, then gave him a hesitant smile. "You are very gracious. I would be delighted by your company, Mr...?"

"Buckshot Roberts, at your service," he said with a humble bow. He pulled out a chair and sat down across from her. Thus began the first true conversation between Buckshot and the raven-haired beauty, Violet.

Late into the night they sat talking. Violet told Buckshot she was a schoolteacher recently arrived in Deadwood, but said little else of her past. Buckshot in turn shared some of his exploits, carefully omitting the darker parts of his history.

When Violet at last stifled a delicate yawn, Buckshot stood. "Please allow me to escort you safely home," he offered. Violet nodded gratefully and allowed him to help her to her feet. Together they stepped out into the cool night air. Only a few drunken stragglers wandered the silent streets.

As they walked slowly through town, Violet slipped her arm through Buckshot's in a familiar fashion that took him aback. He glanced down at her slender hand resting genteelly on his forearm and felt his heart stir in a way it hadn't for a very long time.

At Violet's boarding house they paused awkwardly on the porch. Violet smiled and Buckshot thought he caught a glint of playfulness in her eyes. "My hero," she said softly, then leaned in and planted a delicate kiss on his cheek. Before he could react, she disappeared quickly through the door.

Buckshot stood frozen for a moment, gently touching his face where her lips had been. Then he found himself grinning into the darkness like a fool. Shaking his head, he wandered off into the night, his mind filled with thoughts of Violet's raven hair and sparkling green eyes.

Chapter 3 - Buckshot Roberts Meets Billy the Kid

The next morning, Buckshot rose early and headed to the saloon for some breakfast. He was surprised to find Violet there, seated daintily at the bar. She wore a pretty floral dress and greeted him with a smile. "I hoped I might see you this morning," she said warmly.

Buckshot tipped his hat, suddenly feeling shy. "A fine morning to you, miss." He sat on the stool next to her and ordered coffee and biscuits when the bartender appeared.

"I wanted to thank you again for coming to my aid last night," Violet said, turning her green eyes on Buckshot. "It was a comfort having you there. I feel...safe with you." She laid her hand gently over his, causing Buckshot's heart to skip a beat.

Their breakfast was interrupted by shouts and running feet outside. The sheriff burst into the saloon, face red with panic. "It's McCreedy and his men!" he cried. "They're ridin' this way lookin' for blood!"

Buckshot was on his feet in an instant, his face grim. Violet clutched his arm fearfully. "What will we do?" she whispered. Buckshot took her hands and looked into her eyes. "Stay here," he instructed firmly. Then he strode outside to meet the coming storm.

Riding furiously down the street were a dozen hard-looking men led by the notorious outlaw Jim McCreedy himself. With whoops and hollers, they fired their pistols wildly into the air, spurring their mounts on faster. Anyone in their path fled for cover. It was utter lawlessness.

As the rampaging gang neared the saloon, Buckshot stepped into the middle of the street, once again placing himself squarely in their path. He stood calmly facing down the oncoming riders, feet spread in a shooter's stance. McCreedy pulled up short in front of him, rage twisting his features.

"You must got a death wish, friend," McCreedy growled at Buckshot. "Coming between me and what I aim to take for myself... mighty foolish choice." His men fanned out, circling around to hem Buckshot in.

Buckshot met McCreedy's glare steadily. "This town ain't yours to take," he said. "But you could still ride out and spare it further grief." His hands hung loosely near his holstered Colts, ready to draw at the first sign of violence. The rest of Deadwood seemed to hold its breath.

McCreedy threw back his head and laughed cruelly. "If it's a fight you want, killer, I'll oblige!" In a blur he went for his pistol. Buckshot was faster--two deafening shots rang out and McCreedy was left clutching a bleeding hand.

With a roar, the other cowboys all drew their weapons. The street erupted into chaos as both sides dove for cover and started blasting away at each other. Buckshot darted behind a wagon, bullets kicking up dirt all around him. He took a breath and then spun out, pistols flashing. Two cowboys fell from their saddles before they could get off a shot.

The remaining gang members spurred their horses up and down the street wildly, firing their Winchesters. Windows shattered and wood splinters flew as deadly lead filled the air. From the saloon doorway, Violet watched in horror, helpless to aid the man who fought alone while the rest cowered.

Having emptied his pistols, Buckshot crouched back behind the wagon and hastily reloaded. McCreedy had retreated at the start of the fight but Buckshot knew he wouldn't stay gone for long. As expected, the big outlaw soon came galloping back down the street, firing his rifle one-handed despite his injured hand.

Buckshot leaned out and snapped off several shots, but McCreedy weaved and evaded them. As the distance closed, Buckshot realized McCreedy meant to simply ride right over him. At the last second, he dove aside as McCreedy's horse thundered past, its hooves missing him by inches.

Rolling back to his feet, Buckshot drew and fired again but the enraged McCreedy didn't slow. Wheeling his steed about, he charged again, this time swinging a lariat over his head. As he passed Buckshot, the loop dropped and tightened around Buckshot's gun hand. He was yanked off his feet and dragged along the ground.

Desperately, Buckshot clawed at the ground with his free hand seeking any anchor. At last he grabbed hold of a hitching post and managed to slow to a stop. McCreedy pulled furiously on the rope but Buckshot held firm to the post. Finally with a roar, the outlaw swung out of his saddle and stalked toward Buckshot, drawing a wicked bowie knife.

Seeing McCreedy's approach, Buckshot let go his grip on the post and rolled free of the lariat loop. Coming up with pistols leveled, he tried to fire but the empty clicks told him he was completely out of ammo. McCreedy charged in, slashing viciously with his heavy blade.

Buckshot backed away, narrowly avoiding the knife swipes. He discarded his useless Colts and pulled his own blade to meet

McCreedy's attacks. The two men slashed and parried up and down the street as the remaining gang members shouted encouragement to their boss.

The flashing knives rang as they clashed again and again while the combatants panted and grunted with exertion. Buckshot staggered as McCreedy landed a cut on his left arm but he gritted his teeth and fought on. He had faced worse odds before.

Gradually Buckshot gave ground to McCreedy's relentless assault, luring the big man back toward the saloon. As the outlaw sensed impending triumph, he charged wildly forward. At the last second, Buckshot dodged aside and stuck out a leg to trip his opponent.

McCreedy sprawled headlong into the dirt. Buckshot kicked the knife from his hand and pressed his own blade to McCreedy's throat. "Yield!" Buckshot demanded through ragged breaths. Defeated, the outlaw could only nod sullenly.

Buckshot stepped back warily as McCreedy slowly picked himself up, dust swirling around him. Their eyes locked for a long moment. "This ain't over 'tween us two," McCreedy promised darkly. Then he whistled sharply and swung up into his saddle, shouting for his gang to ride out of Deadwood.

Silence descended on the street. Buckshot sagged back against the saloon wall, exhausted. The cuts on his arm and hands now made themselves known fiercely. But he had survived the storm once again.

The saloon doors pushed open and Violet rushed out to embrace him fiercely. "I thought I'd lost you!" she exclaimed. Pulling back, her face fell as she took in his battered appearance. "You're hurt!"

Despite the pain, Buckshot found himself distracted by her closeness and intoxicating scent. "Just some scratches, ma'am," he said softly. "Nothing too serious." Violet helped him inside where she could tend gently to his wounds.

After having his injuries cleaned and bound, Buckshot gulped some whiskey for the pain. The saloon was empty save for him and Violet. As she placed a cool hand against his cheek, he winced. "Why risk so much for a town not your own?" she asked curiously.

Buckshot looked into her green eyes. "I reckon everybody ought have the chance to build themselves a decent, honest life," he said gravely. "Even an old sinner like me knows that much." Violet gazed back at him with an expression he couldn't quite read.

Their intimacy was broken by the saloon doors swinging open. Buckshot turned quickly, expecting more of McCreedy's men. But it was the sheriff, along with a contingent of townsfolk. Their eyes were wide as they took in the battle-scarred street and saloon. The sheriff let out a low whistle. "Dang it all, Buckshot, we owe you a debt of gratitude!" he declared. "Battling the McCreedy gang single-handed!" The townsfolk murmured their hearty agreement and thanks.

Buckshot just nodded, wincing again as he moved his injured arm. "Weren't nothing, just had to be done is all," he muttered, shying away from their praise. He had only acted on instinct, not out of selflessness. The others didn't need to make him out a hero. Violet placed a hand gently on his shoulder in understanding.

That afternoon, the town doctor checked Buckshot's wounds and bandaged him up properly. Afterwards, Buckshot retired to his room at the hotel to recuperate. Despite the pain, he soon dozed off from sheer exhaustion. His dreams were fitful, full of fire and blood and screams...

A knock at his door woke him sometime after dark. Cautiously, he cracked it open to see Violet standing there in the hall. "I'm sorry to disturb you," she said hesitantly. "Only I couldn't stop worrying, and wished to see you were alright..."

Buckshot opened the door fully to admit her. "No need for apologies, ma'am." In truth, he was touched by her concern. He lit an oil lamp as she glanced around the sparse little room. Her eyes flickered over his holstered Colts on the nightstand. If she had any fear of him, she did not show it.

"Please sit, make yourself comfortable," Buckshot offered politely, taking one of the rickety chairs himself. Violet arranged her skirts and sat delicately on the end of the bed. For a moment they simply looked at each other in the dim light.

"You have shown me only kindness since we met," Violet said finally. "I must confess, when I first saw you, I assumed you were...dangerous. But your actions prove otherwise."

Buckshot looked away, ashamed. "I ain't no angel, Violet," he said heavily. "I done...terrible things..." His voice trailed off, unable to continue. Violet leaned forward and took his rough, calloused hand in her own soft one.

"The past does not define us," she said gently. "What matters is the person you choose to be now." Her faith in him was humbling. They talked long into the night, slowly opening up, sharing hopes and secrets neither had voiced to anyone before.

It was near dawn when Buckshot finally walked Violet back to her boarding house. At the step, she smiled demurely at him. "Thank you for the lovely evening, sir," she said in a teasing formal tone, then laughed. The sound melted Buckshot's heart.

Over the next few days, Violet tended Buckshot's healing wounds. When he was able, they passed many more hours together, strolling through town or sitting conversing quietly as they grew closer. Buckshot had never known such simple joy. For the first time, he allowed himself to believe in second chances.

One morning several days later, Buckshot entered the saloon and sensed something amiss. Conversations stopped abruptly at his appearance. Eyes cut away nervously. He frowned, suspicious now. "Alright, what's going on?" he demanded gruffly.

The sheriff looked very uncomfortable. "Well now, Buckshot, ain't no cause for alarm," he said, raising his hands placatingly. "Only...McCreedy and his gang rode back into town earlier." Buckshot tensed, ready to charge out and confront the outlaws.

The sheriff quickly moved to stop him. "Hold on now! They ain't here to make trouble! They're over to the assayers office, selling off a big bag of gold nuggets. Seems they found themselves a rich claim up in the hills."

Buckshot's eyes narrowed, sensing deception. "Since when do those vipers go digging in the dirt like prospectors?" He took a step toward the door but the sheriff blocked him.

"Now listen here, you done enough! Me and the deputies can keep the peace from here on." The lawman put a hand on Buckshot's chest, desperation in his voice. "McCreedy promised no more trouble if we let him be. Just let it lie!"

Buckshot stood rigid, hands curling into fists. He knew leaving McCreedy alone was a mistake. But clearly no one here had any stomach left for a fight. They would happily lap up whatever lies that snake told them if it meant a quiet life. With great effort, Buckshot forced himself to relax and give a curt nod. It took every ounce of willpower to turn and walk away rather than confront McCreedy directly. The sheriff sighed in great relief.

Outside, Buckshot paced in agitation, trying to decide on his next move. He refused to trust that viper McCreedy's word of peace. His thoughts were interrupted by cries of his name. Turning, he saw Violet rushing up to him, face flushed prettily from running. His grim demeanor faded at the sight of her.

"I'm so pleased to see you out and about," Violet said brightly. "And you seem fully healed now, thanks heaven!" She tucked her arm in his happily. Despite his concerns, Buckshot couldn't suppress a smile. "Right as rain," he assured her.

As they walked, Violet chattered light-heartedly about the upcoming Founders Day festival and dance. But Buckshot found it hard to focus. His thoughts kept straying back to McCreedy's gang and their dubious claims of discovering gold. He remained uneasy.

Sensing his distraction, Violet stopped and turned him gently to face her. "What is it?" she asked, studying his eyes searchingly. "I can see something weighs on your mind."

Buckshot hesitated before answering slowly. "I don't trust that McCreedy has given up his crusade against this town," he admitted. "But folks here are ready to believe his lies for peace. I...don't know what to do for the best anymore." He despised indecision and self-doubt.

Violet stepped close and placed a hand softly on his cheek. "You have already done so much for this place. No one expects more of you. Whatever happens next is not solely your responsibility." Her compassion touched him deeply. Nodding slowly, Buckshot covered her delicate hand with his own callused one. No words were needed.

They resumed their stroll, Buckshot feeling considerably lighter. As they passed the town's small white-steepled church, he heard the preacher from before speaking passionately within about walking the righteous path. Buckshot thought again on the man's words of non-violence and faith. Perhaps he had been too quick to dismiss the power of such things.

That evening, the saloon was lively once more. Buckshot sat with Violet, trying to push his nagging worries away for the moment. Nearby, a handsome stranger poker game drew a crowd betting enthusiastically and shouting encouragement to the players.

One gambler stood out from the rough types around him. He was boyish and slight, dressed neatly in black with a beaded buckskin jacket. But the self-assuredness with which he handled the cards and chips suggested plenty of experience. Piles of money stacked up before him as he raked in hand after hand.

A hush fell over the onlookers as the young gambler neatly spread a full house on the table and reached to pull the substantial pot towards himself. "Well played, kid," chuckled the gruff older miner across from him good-naturedly as he tossed his cards down in defeat.

"Much obliged, friend," said the young man with an easy grin as he stacked his new winnings. His voice was smooth, almost pretty. "Your deal." As the miner passed the deck for cutting, the gambler deftly flipped three aces off the bottom into his waiting palm in a move that drew gasps of astonishment from the crowd. Buckshot shook his head, equally impressed by the kid's sleight of hand.

"Kid, you sure got some magic in them fingers," laughed the miner. "What's your handle?" The young gambler paused his shuffling and tipped his hat cordially to the room. "Name's William Bonney," he said. "But folks 'round here mostly call me Billy. Billy the Kid."

At the sound of that notorious moniker, Buckshot sat bolt upright in surprise and recognition. Scanning the youthful features more closely, he now saw the same cocksure gunslinger who had built a bloody reputation as a vigilante in the Lincoln County range war over in New Mexico territory. Rumor had it Billy the Kid had fled east after being involved in the murder of a sheriff there. So this was the famous outlaw, though he scarcely looked old enough to shave.

Noticing Buckshot's intense interest, Billy flashed him a cocky wink. "Care to join our game, friend?" he asked, raising an eyebrow. "Ten dollar buy-in."

Buckshot was sorely tempted to take the brash young punk down a peg or two, but thought better of it. Best not to stir up trouble needlessly. He shook his head politely. "Much obliged for the offer, but I'm just fine spectating this evening."

Billy shrugged and returned to his cards. But his gaze kept flicking back to Buckshot between hands, as if sensing a worthy opponent. For his part, Buckshot remained subtly alert to the newcomer's presence, fingertips drifting occasionally near his holstered Colts. Violet kept a wary eye on the young gunslinger as well, her brow creased in concern.

After winning another large hand, Billy stretched and excused himself from the poker game. As he sauntered to the bar for a whiskey, he made deliberate eye contact with Buckshot and raised his glass in salute. Message received. Clearly the cocky youth wanted to size up the veteran gunfighter. Sipping his drink slowly, Billy scanned the room in a way that seemed casual but missed nothing. His hand never strayed far from the Colt on his hip.

Despite the subtle tension, Buckshot had to admire the kid's composure and confidence. At that age he himself had been full of piss and vinegar too. Taken less experienced men by surprise, until the law caught up with him. But Billy the Kid had managed to evade consequences so far, it seemed. The day would come, though. It always did.

As Billy turned to leave, he paused and met Buckshot's gaze directly for the first time. "Pleasure making your acquaintance," he said with a gentlemanly tip of his hat. "I expect we'll be seeing each other again." Touching a finger to the brim again, he sauntered from the saloon. The batwing

The batwing doors swung slowly in Billy's wake. Buckshot watched him go thoughtfully. The kid clearly had reputation and ability, but something about his cockiness didn't sit quite right. He resolved to keep an eye on the young gunslinger during his time in Deadwood.

Turning back to Violet, he saw her frown had deepened. Gently, Buckshot asked "What is it that troubles you, my dear?"

Violet lowered her voice. "I have heard stories of that Billy the Kid and the crimes he's committed. He is dangerous." She shivered slightly.

Buckshot patted her hand reassuringly. "Now, don't you worry none. I ain't about to let some upstart with a reputation hurt anybody in this town."

Still, Violet seemed unsettled. The encounter had soured the mood of their evening. Not long after, Buckshot escorted her home under the starry night sky. At her door, she faced him, the worry still evident in her eyes.

"Please be cautious," she implored him. "I couldn't bear..." She didn't finish the thought. Buckshot just smiled and tipped her chin up. "This old boy's been in tighter scrapes afore," he said lightly. "I'll be just fine." Violet smiled back bravely. Then, moving onto her tiptoes, she kissed him softly on the lips. Buckshot was too stunned to react before she disappeared inside. He walked away grinning foolishly.

The next morning, Buckshot heard that Billy and his gang had gotten into a vicious brawl at the smaller saloon across town. A man had been shot, but luckily survived. It was the sort of reckless violence Billy the Kid was known for. Buckshot's instincts told him the worst was yet to come.

He found Billy loitering on the hotel porch later, chatting up a pretty young serving girl. As Buckshot approached, Billy took his leave of the giggling girl and turned to him with a cocky grin. "Morning to you, sir," Billy greeted with false formality. "Been hearing tales of your exploits about town. Color me impressed."

Buckshot got right to the point. "Seems your boys started some unrest last night. Man's lucky to be alive, way I heard it." He eyed Billy evenly.

Billy shrugged, unconcerned. "Just a minor dispute that got out of hand is all. No need to get your dander up." He smiled disarmingly. "I promise we'll be on our best behavior from here on."

"See that you do," Buckshot said coldly. "I'll be keeping my own watch, regardless." Turning on his heel, he walked away before Billy could respond. The sound of the kid's laughter followed him down the street. Buckshot's hands flexed in anger, but he maintained control. That cocky punk would slip up soon enough.

Over the next few days, Billy and his gang rode out of town regularly on mysterious errands. They would return laden with full saddlebags that clinked suspiciously. When whispers spread that they had been sticking up gold shipments from the mines, Buckshot again confronted Billy outside the saloon.

"I done warned you to stay out of trouble," he growled, cornering the young outlaw. "Now I hear you're robbing and plundering openly." His hand drifted toward his holstered Colt.

Billy's easy smile didn't waver. "Buckshot, friend, you seem to have gotten some bad information," he said smoothly. "My boys and I have been trying our luck panning upstream. What we do with our hard earned findings is our own affair." His eyes glinted dangerously beneath the charming veneer.

With great effort, Buckshot restrained himself from wiping the smirk off Billy's face. It would only lead to more bloodshed. "This is the last time I'll ask nicely," he said in a low voice. "Take your crew and clear out by week's end. Or there will be trouble."

Turning on his heel, Buckshot strode away as Billy called mockingly after him.

That Saturday was the Founders Day festival and dance. Decorations were hung on every building and tantalizing smells wafted from the chuck wagons. Musicians tuned their fiddles as anticipation built. It was a pleasant diversion from the looming threat.

When Buckshot arrived to pick up Violet for the dance, she took his breath away in a pale blue satin dress. "You look ravishing, my dear," he said, kissing her hand. She smiled radiantly and took his arm. Buckshot felt like the luckiest man there.

The townsfolk were in high spirits, drinking and merrymaking. Even Buckshot allowed himself to relax and enjoy the festivities, Violet on his arm. They danced gracefully, ate heartily, and laughed together like not a care existed. For those few hours, the shadow cast by Billy the Kid and his gang seemed very far away.

As dusk fell, Violet rested her head contently on Buckshot's shoulder as they slowly revolved on the dance floor. Gazing into her bright eyes, Buckshot was filled with a soaring happiness he had never expected to find. No words were needed in that moment.

When the music ended, Buckshot led Violet from the press of dancers toward the edge of the lantern light. Finding an empty bench beneath a tree, they sat together looking up at the glittering night sky. Violet snuggled closer against Buckshot's side, shivering slightly in the cool air. He drew her near and she rested her head on his chest with a sigh of perfect contentment.

Tilting her face up to his, Violet's eyes were luminous in the moonlight. "No one has ever made me feel this way," she whispered. Their lips met in a lingering kiss. Time itself seemed to halt. Buckshot knew then that he loved this woman with all that he was. He silently vowed to protect her and their future together, whatever it took.

Gunshots suddenly split the still night air, followed by wild whoops and hollers. Buckshot was instantly on his feet, whirling toward the commotion with guns drawn. Across the field, he saw shadows on horseback careening drunkenly through the festival chaos, firing pistols into the air. It was Billy and his gang, intent on ruining the town's celebration.

Buckshot turned swiftly back to Violet who stared after him with frightened eyes. "Go home now and bar your door," he told her urgently. "I promise you, this ends tonight." Giving her hand one last squeeze, he raced off toward the rowdy outlaws with vengeance in his heart. The final showdown between Buckshot and Billy the Kid was at hand.

Chapter 4 - Showdown at High Noon

Buckshot stalked determinately through the disrupted Founders Day festivities, one hand resting menacingly on a holstered pistol. All around him people were fleeing in panic as Billy the Kid and his gang whooped drunkenly, firing their guns into the air. The outlaws were riding up and down recklessly, terrorizing anyone in their path. It was time for someone to take a stand.

Drawing near to the vandals, Buckshot stepped directly into the path of Billy's horse. "That's enough!" he yelled fiercely. "Your terror ends tonight!" His steely gaze locked with Billy's glazed eyes. The young outlaw just laughed mockingly and spurred his horse on straight at Buckshot.

At the last second, Buckshot threw himself aside to avoid getting trampled. As Billy raced past, he lashed out with a boot, catching Billy hard in the knee. The young outlaw cursed as he was nearly unseated from the saddle. Reigning his horse around sharply, Billy drew his Colt and fired wildly at Buckshot.

Buckshot dove and rolled, narrowly dodging the reckless shots. Coming up with pistols in both hands, he snapped off four quick rounds. Billy yelped as a bullet creased his arm, causing him to drop his own gun. Furious, the outlaw wheeled his horse again and took off with Buckshot blasting away after him.

As he reloaded on the run, Buckshot saw two of Billy's men up ahead, tugging a screaming young woman into an alley. With fiery determination, he rushed the men and pistol-whipped one from his saddle before turning the gun on the other, forcing him to release the frightened woman. "Git on home now! Go!" he yelled and she fled to safety.

The rest of Billy's gang was circling back around, guns blazing. Buckshot sprinted for cover, bullets kicking up dirt on all sides. As he slid into a narrow gap between two buildings, more shots sent splinters flying right over his head. He was pinned down.

Thinking fast, Buckshot ripped a lit lantern from a nearby porch and hurled it onto an empty wagon. The oil ignited with a whoosh, spooking the horses tied to the wagon. The panicked animals broke free and charged straight for the gang members with flaming eyes and manes. Cursing loudly, the outlaws scattered before the raging steeds.

Buckshot pressed the distraction, moving up behind and blasting away with his pistols. One gang member fell wounded from his horse while two more had their hats shot clear off their heads. The others quickly galloped for cover while returning fire wildly. Their initial bravado was fading fast.

Suddenly a new group of riders came charging onto the chaotic scene - it was the sheriff and his posse! "Throw down them guns, you hoodlums!" the sheriff bellowed. Without their leader Billy urging them on, the remaining gang members quickly surrendered to the lawmen. The tide had turned.

Leaving the outlaws to the sheriff, Buckshot went after the one who mattered - Billy himself. Following the sounds of raucous laughter, he tracked the cocky outlaw to the saloon. Bursting through the doors with pistols leveled, he spotted Billy harassing the terrified bartender. "Party's over, Kid!" Buckshot yelled. "Let's settle this man to man."

Spinning drunkenly to face him, Billy grinned recklessly. "Well, if it ain't the man himself!" he declared, swaggering forwards. "Come to put me in my place, huh? Give it your best shot then, old man!" He reached clumsily for his own empty holster before realizing his gun was gone.

Seeing Billy's mistake, the bartender nervously picked up the discarded Colt from the bar and offered it to Billy. The outlaw paused, swaying. "Well now, that's right neighborly of you," Billy exclaimed in surprise, taking back the pistol. He turned unsteadily to face Buckshot again. "Your move, pardner."

Buckshot hesitated, unwilling to gun down this cocky fool in cold blood, armed or not. But he knew Billy had no such compulsion. Keeping his pistols trained on the outlaw, Buckshot spoke evenly through gritted teeth. "Kid, you got two ways out of this fight. The easy way is you walk free without that iron you're holdin'. But we both know you ain't gonna choose that road."

Billy barked out a laugh and shook his head. "You know me too well already, old timer." He drew himself up straighter and steadied his grip on the Colt. "So let's get to the part we both been waiting for. High noon tomorrow in the street. Just you and me." A glint of anticipation had crept into his glazed eyes. The bartender paled and looked pleadingly at Buckshot, but he just nodded grimly. Nothing left but the final reckoning now.

As Buckshot turned to leave, Billy called after him. "And Buckshot - don't get cold feet and try to light out tonight. I'll hunt you to the ends of the earth if you rob me of my rightful glory." Holding the whiskey bottle aloft like a victory cup, the wild outlaw whooped loudly then collapsed into a chair. Tomorrow's duel weighed heavy on Buckshot's mind as he walked slowly from the saloon. So be it.

It was a restless night for Buckshot. At dawn, he rose quietly and prepared. His pistols were cleaned and loaded methodically. His black suit was neatly pressed, white shirt bright against it. At last Buckshot slipped on his holster and drew a Colt from it, testing the smooth spin of the cylinder. He was as ready as he could be.

Stepping outside into the cool morning air, Buckshot sucked in a deep breath. The rising sun already burned away the haze, promising a scorching day ahead. Fitting weather for the task at hand. With deliberate strides, Buckshot headed for town and destiny.

Few souls were out and about so early. But word seemed to have spread. As he neared the main street, people began peeking from windows and doors before gathering cautiously to watch from the boardwalk. Whispers followed Buckshot as he passed by without acknowledging the onlookers. This was between him and Billy now.

Towards the far end of the street, a lone figure stepped from the saloon into the middle of the dusty road. Billy the Kid stood waiting, hands hitched casually near his holstered Colt. To either side, people quickly moved back towards the buildings, not wanting to be caught in the crossfire. A hush fell over the scene, until the only sound was the lonely creaking of a sign in the morning breeze. Two men faced off, but only one would walk away.

With steady strides Buckshot moved forward until he was twenty paces from Billy. There he halted and turned to face the cocky young outlaw who had finally pushed his luck too far. Billy stared back with that defiant grin, coiled and ready for the draw. A slight morning breeze ruffled his dark mop of hair beneath the tilted hat. He had dressed up for his own funeral.

For a handful of seconds the two gunfighters stood frozen, eyes locked, hands ready. The world seemed to hold its breath. Then Billy moved, lightning fast. But Buckshot was already in motion, muscle memory honed from countless prior duels take over. Two shots roared out deafeningly, drowning out the cries of onlookers. Acrid gun smoke swirled, temporarily concealing the outcome.

As the haze cleared, Buckshot remained standing - Billy had missed clean. But the kid himself was staggering backward, clutching a spreading crimson stain on his side. Buckshot had only wounded, unwilling to take the cocky fool's life directly. Groaning through gritted teeth, Billy half-fell against a hitching post, leaving a red smear down the aged wood.

Buckshot calmly reloaded his single spent round, then holstered his Colt. The watching crowd murmured anxiously but remained at a distance. His gaze never leaving Billy, Buckshot spoke in a tone of quiet authority that carried down the silent street.

"It's over Kid. You're through in this town. Get patched up and move on down the trail, and we'll leave it at that. Man to man." He hesitated, then added more gently, "Ain't no more need for killing today."

Billy glared back at him with a mix of bitterness and grudging respect. Then, grunting painfully, he began limping away aided by a pair of his men who emerged hesitantly from the saloon. Before disappearing inside again, Billy turned to tip his hat wordlessly to Buckshot with his good arm. Message received. There would be no further trouble from him today.

As the dust settled over the street, a murmur ran through the crowd. Buckshot had put in its place the notorious outlaw that none had dared stand up to before. Their relief and joy was palpable. Smiling faces pushed forward, hands reaching to shake Buckshot's gratefully. His normally shy manner had no place given their outpouring of gratitude.

Searching the crowd anxiously, Buckshot at last laid eyes on Violet's beloved face. As their gaze met, her expression transformed from anxious worry to deepest affection and pride. They moved together without need for words. Buckshot laid his calloused palm softly against Violet's delicate cheek. Her joyful smile was all that mattered to him now with the threat ended. Tomorrow could wait - this moment was theirs.

News spread fast of the dramatic showdown. By sundown of that High Noon, Billy the Kid and his remaining gang had retreated from Deadwood, never to return. Though it rankled Billy's pride to back down, he recognized when he was beat fair and square. There were easier pickings to be had elsewhere.

With the outlaws gone, an atmosphere of jubilation took over the town. Drinks flowed freely in the saloon that night as Buckshot's health was toasted over and over by increasingly drunken well-wishers. Tales of the duel grew more exaggerated with each telling, but Buckshot just chuckled and let them have their fun. All he cared was enjoying a quiet celebratory drink with Violet by his side.

Later, beneath a clear night sky bright with stars, Buckshot walked Violet home. At her porch they embraced tenderly, both thankful for the peace that had been too long lacking. As Buckshot gazed into his beloved's sparkling eyes, he was filled with deep contentment. The future brimmed with possibility for them both.

"Will you come for supper tomorrow at my home?" Violet asked softly, a playful smile dancing on her lips. "I should like to make a proper gentleman of you yet." Laughing joyfully, Buckshot swept her up and spun her around before kissing her full on the mouth. "My darling, wild horses couldn't keep me away," he declared. With a smile that melted his heart, Violet bid her hero goodnight.

The next evening Buckshot tidied his rugged appearance up as best he was able before arriving on Violet's doorstep with wildflowers in hand. She welcomed him in with a radiant smile and kiss on the cheek that left him flushed. Just sitting beside her for a meal felt greater happiness than Buckshot had ever expected to have.

Over the next weeks and months, they passed many more blissful evenings together as Buckshot was nursed back to full health in body and spirit by Violet's loving care. Slowly the raw memories from his violent past were soothed. He no longer woke in a cold sweat from nightmares, reaching for a pistol. Violet's gentle presence returned meaning to his existence. Buckshot came to understand peace for the first time.

On a golden afternoon fragrant with lilac blossoms, Buckshot worked up the courage to propose to Violet properly beneath their special willow tree. When she joyfully accepted, laughing through tears of happiness, Buckshot thought his heart might burst from sheer joy. Holding his blushing bride-to-be close, he sighed in contentment. This was heaven on earth.

They were wed in a modest ceremony at the small white-steepled church on the edge of town. Buckshot wore his only suit, mended for the occasion. Violet was radiant in her mother's antique lace gown that had traveled west by wagon. Only a handful of well-wishers were in attendance, but that was all they desired.

Exchanging their heartfelt vows, the once wayward gunslinger and the kind-hearted woman who saw the good in his battered soul pledged themselves to one another for eternity. Sealed with a kiss full of promise, they turned hand in hand to face the future together without trepidation. This righteously joyful union heralded a new beginning for Buckshot. Whatever came their way, they would meet it as one.

The humble churchyard wedding was but the start of their new life journey. Afterwards, friends cheered the smiling couple on to a celebratory dinner. A fiddler played merrily while guests ate, drank, and laughed well into the starry night. Gone was the troubled aura that had plagued the town - in its place there was now hope.

Swept up in the merriment, Buckshot twirled his beaming bride exuberantly on the makeshift dance floor to the fiddler's joyous tune. Her dark hair fanned out as she spun, face glowing and eyes only for her beloved. As the music ended, Buckshot dipped Violet back dramatically, earning cheers from their genteel audience. Righting her again, he gazed into her sparkling eyes and stroked her soft cheek. In Violet's loving companionship, Buckshot had found the purpose that redeems any man.

Later, arms entwined beneath that giant cottonwood by the creek's chuckling water, husband and wife shared a perfect first kiss as man and wife. No sweeter moment had ever passed for Buckshot than holding Violet in the dappled moonlight. He silently vowed to do right by his new family from here on. The trials of the past were well and truly behind them both. What lay ahead now was a blank page, theirs to fill.

As weeks turned to months, Buckshot settled into married life more readily than he could have dreamed. Together they made a cozy home filled with laughter, companionship and dreams of the years to come. His days of solitude on the range now seemed a distant memory. At Violet's side, Buckshot had found his true place in this world. Come darkness or storm, they would weather it gladly side by side.

On a golden summer afternoon nine months after their wedding, Violet went into labor. Buckshot was banished to anxious pacing outside their bedroom door as her pained cries sounded within. When at last the lusty wailing of an infant pierced the air, he burst in to behold Violet cradling their precious daughter, Rosie. Buckshot dropped to his knees at the bedside overcome with awe and joy at this new life they had created. Their family was now complete.

In the years that followed, Buckshot savored his new role as devoted husband and father. Each dawn when little Rosie came bounding into their bedroom to rouse her Pa for adventures, his heart surged anew. Her tiny hand clasped in his brought a rightness he had never known. With his girls to live for, Buckshot walked tall. The future was a boundless country begging for them to explore it together.

Rosie grew more each day, her laughter infectious, spirit unbreakable. Buckshot nurtured her curiosity about the world, answering her endless questions patiently. When she was scared, his arms were her sanctuary. As she got older, he taught her to ride, fish, shoot and stand up for herself. Under her father's loving guidance, Rosie flourished free and dauntless.

At day's end, Buckshot would lift his sleepy girl to carry her inside to Violet. Their little family gathered close on the porch watching the brilliant colors paint the western horizon. A contented silence reigned. Buckshot's heart was so full of gratitude for the family and honest life he had found in this place, beyond anything he deserved. With his wife's hand held in his, their child nodding off in his lap, Buckshot was fulfilled.

Seasons passed serenely one into the next. Buckshot never ceased to cherish each new day with Violet and their growing daughter. The years had weathered his face, but his back remained straight, spirit undimmed. He still cut an imposing figure around town, but now folk greeted him as friend rather than dangerous stranger. For the first time in memory, he knew community.

A decade after exchanging their vows, when the cottonwoods blazed gold in the crisp autumn air, Buckshot was blessed with a son to carry on his name. As he cradled the squalling babe, tears of joy standing in his eyes, Violet squeezed his arm. "He has your fire," she said knowingly. Their family was now complete.

In the golden twilight years of Buckshot's life, as he watched his children grow, marry and have little ones of their own, his cup overflowed with blessings uncounted. Surrounded by his proud and loving family, the once lonely gunslinger knew a happiness greater than he ever could have dreamed in those wayward days of youth. Now in his beloved's tender embrace each night, Buckshot rested easy. There were no more dragons left to face in this life. Every good thing he had done or been was because Violet saw the light in him when all others cast him asunder. She was his sanctuary, his redemption, his guiding star back to grace. With her hand in his, Buckshot stepped forward joyfully into eternity, made whole at last.

Chapter 5 - Buckshot Roberts's Past Life as a Lawman

On a clear morning some weeks after the showdown with Billy the Kid, Buckshot rose before dawn as was his habit. After stoking the fire, he sat sipping coffee slowly as the first light crept across the floorboards. Violet still slept peacefully in their bed, dark hair splayed across her pillow. Buckshot watched her fondly, hardly believing his good fortune.

Presently, Violet began to stir. Sitting up drowsily, she smiled as her eyes met Buckshot's across the small room. "Good morning, my love," she said softly. Buckshot crossed to her and planted a kiss on her forehead. "And to you, my darling," he replied. As Violet rose to dress for the day ahead, his heart swelled with love for her.

Over a simple breakfast of eggs and bacon from the iron skillet, Buckshot asked what Violet's plans were as he headed out for the day's work. "I shall catch up on some reading," she said, "and then visit the mercantile for goods." After Buckshot impressed on her to take care in town, they parted ways with a lingering kiss.

Striding down the dusty main street toward the livery stable, Buckshot touched two fingers to the brim of his hat in greeting the few townsfolk out and about their early business. Though once seen as a dangerous gunslinger, he was now accepted as one of their own. Buckshot aimed to keep the trust he had been shown in this place that he and Violet now called home.

At the livery, he prepared his pinto horse that had been his steady companion these long years on the trail. As Buckshot swung into the saddle and turned the horse's head towards the plains beyond town, he felt that familiar thrill that had drawn him to the unfettered life of a cowboy since youth. This land called to his restless spirit.

Riding out past the last buildings, Buckshot relaxed into an easy rhythm with his mount. The pinto knew the way having been this route many times over their years together. Beyond the dusty town, an expanse of gently rolling prairie stretched as far as the eye could see to distant blue mountains. This was cattle country, wide open and full of possibility if a man was willing to work for it. The frontier spirit still held sway here.

Topping a rise, Buckshot gazed out across wave after wave of grasslands interspersed with groves of cottonwoods and willow following water's meandering trail. A hawk circled high above riding the updraft, also surveying the bounty below. Somewhere out in this vastness was the herd he had been hired to manage. Owned by a cattle baron who had ambitions of building an empire across the territory, but no kin interested in seeing it done. Men like Buckshot made it happen.

After some miles the cattle finally appeared, a mass of mottled brown and black spread out across a flat grazing contently on the sweet grass. Most raised their heads incuriously as Buckshot loped through their midst, checking for signs of sickness or injury. Satisfied the herd was faring well, he guided his mount to a vantage point where he could observe their movement across the savanna. The pinto lowered its head gratefully to crop at the prairie grass, unbothered by the endless bovine sea. From his elevated perch, Buckshot kept a watchful eye for predators or wayward steers. This was his peace – solitude on the open range caring for the herd. The honest work spoke to his soul.

As the sun traversed its arc overhead, the cattle carried on lazily. Buckshot shifted in the saddle, bones and muscles protesting the long hours astride despite years adapting to the life. He was no longer a young man, though still hardened by the years. Gazing out at the ocean of grass, he recalled when it had all begun...

Buckshot – though that was not the name he carried then – had been a rambunctious youth with big dreams but little chance to achieve them. His home life was difficult, and he struggled to stay on the right path despite the easy lures of trouble. When eventually it became too much to bear, he fled West chasing freedom and opportunity.

After a brief stint panning fruitlessly for gold, he signed on as a ranch hand at an outfit south of Santa Fe. The work was exhausting but honest, and he took pride in learning the ways of caring for the herd. In time he gained a reputation around the territory as a skilled cowhand who could be trusted with the boss's stock.

When trouble came, as it always did in those parts, Buckshot's steady head and good moral compass made him the natural choice to pin on the Sheriff's star. As newly sworn lawman, he found purpose maintaining order in their corner of the untamed land. The sheriff's office became a refuge against his own lingering demons. His star drew a line he dare not cross, keeping temptation at bay.

Inevitably his principles were tested when a vicious band of outlaws known as the Dry Gulch boys descended on the region. They left ravaged homesteads and outgunned lawmen in their wake, growing bolder with each score. Every other enforcer in the territory refused to stand up to them, but Buckshot would not cower when duty called. Perhaps he was foolishly naïve not to see the tragedy looming.

After months tracking the gang's movements, Buckshot finally learned their plans to rob the assayers office in Santa Fe before fleeing south across the border for good. He dispatched urgent telegrams urging help in intercepting the gang. The day of reckoning had come at last. Young and emboldened with righteousness on his side, Buckshot rode for Santa Fe alone when no backup materialized. There he would make his stand.

As expected, the Dry Gulch boys hit the assay office hard and fast that afternoon. Buckshot confronted them alone in the dusty street with pistols drawn and orders to surrender. For a moment the outlaws hesitated, torn between making a run for it or attempting to muscle through this solitary lawman. But their leader just laughed harshly, sensing opportunity to grow his legend further. Buckshot had stared down the devil, and the devil had not blinked.

When the smoke and chaos cleared, four gang members lay dead in the street from Buckshot's blazing guns. But he took a slug to the shoulder that left his own shooting arm hanging limp. Weaponless and gravely injured, he was no match for the furious outlaw leader stalking towards him with vengeance in his eyes. But just then, hoofbeats signaled the long-awaited posse thundering onto the scene with guns ablaze!

It was over in seconds once outnumbered. The remaining gang members were cut down or surrendered. Only the leader made a desperate run for it, knife drawn and murder in his heart. He almost reached Buckshot before several lawmen fired in unison to put him down for good. Thus the scourge of the Dry Gulch gang ended in hot blood and gunsmoke.

Later, as the dust settled over the grisly scene, Buckshot learned how fortune had smiled on him that fateful day. The telegraph wires had been down for hours, so no help had received word of his stand. But a brave stationmaster rode through the night to spread the call in person once the wires came back up. That timely courage had saved Buckshot's life when all seemed lost.

In the aftermath, once his shoulder healed, Buckshot gained notoriety across the territory for daring to confront the vicious gang alone, buying time for justice to arrive. The sheriff's star no longer felt a burden but a badge of honor. But the mantle of lawman began to chafe against his independent spirit. After a time Buckshot drifted on again following the lure of the horizon. Of course that youthful impetuousness led him down a darker trail eventually...

A soft nicker from his pinto brought Buckshot back from the bittersweet memories of his life before this place. Shaking off the reverie, he peered out to watch the herd again but saw no cause for alarm. Dusk was approaching now, the sun sinking slowly behind distant hills. It was time to start moving the cattle back closer to town where the hands could watch them for the night.

With a sharp whistle and heel nudge, Buckshot urged his mount down towards the milling herd. At his approach, the cattle began plodding together in the direction he aimed them. The ride back was accompanied by bawling calves searching for their mothers amidst the sea of shuffling bovine bodies. But the herd remained calm under Buckshot's steady guidance. He felt a deep satisfaction in a good day's work.

By the time the lights of Deadwood finally came into view, flickering warmly against the night sky, Buckshot was weary to the bone. Despite his sore muscles, he stayed vigilant until the cattle were safely situated in the enclosed pasture with fresh water and hay. Only then did he unsaddle his pinto in the familiar livery, wipe the trusty beast down, and turn him into a stall with an affectionate pat for his stalwart companion. That done, Buckshot trudged gratefully towards home and Violet's loving embrace.

Over dinner together, Violet chatted happily about her day in town as Buckshot savored the venison stew, sopping up the last drops with a chunk of bread. The simple comforts of hearth and home still felt slightly foreign after so many years adrift and alone. But it was a feeling he could now never be without. Their cozy life together was a harbor after too long spent being battered about by storms and lured by siren songs onto jagged shoals. Here at last was a safe landing.

Later, as they lay entwined beneath the quilts, Violet ran a hand gently across Buckshot's weathered face. "Your mind has been wandering someplace far from here today," she murmured. He smiled ruefully. She knew him better than he knew himself at times. He shared with her then of the memories stirred up on the prairie.

Violet listened intently, her eyes never leaving his. "Do not let the shadows of the past darken the light we have found," she whispered when he had finished. Drawing her near, Buckshot kissed her tenderly. She was right of course. The lost years stretched behind him, but their future lay ahead bright with promise. Whatever was to come, they would walk forward together without regret. With that peace in his heart, Buckshot slept soundly, the warm weight of Violet in his arms anchoring him close.

Chapter 6 - Billy the Kid's Life of Crime

A few weeks had passed since Buckshot's showdown with Billy the Kid when a letter arrived that would change everything.

It was from an old friend, Sheriff Brady, requesting help tracking down Billy yet again. The Kid had resurfaced in New Mexico and was forming a new gang. Brady was desperate to stop the outlaw before he could ignite another reign of terror across the territory. He implored Buckshot to join the hunt, knowing there were few men as skilled at running down dangerous fugitives.

At first Buckshot was reluctant - he had left those raw days behind him and finally carved out an honest life here with Violet. But the more he considered it, the more he felt compelled to finish what had started that day in the Deadwood street. Billy was a rabid coyote that needed putting down permanent before he ruined more lives. And who better to see it done than the man who had bested him once already. That night Buckshot broke the news to Violet that duty called him away for a spell. Predictably she was distraught, but even she could see the fire in his eyes. Buckshot would ride at dawn.

Traveling fast and light, Buckshot made good time heading south as Sheriff Brady's letter directed. The miles sped by in a creak of saddle leather and drumbeat of hooves. He stuck to the wild country, avoiding towns where word of his coming might precede him. Alone on the trail again, Buckshot was surprised to find he felt more purpose than loneliness this journey. For the first time, he rode for more than just himself.

After two hard weeks on the trail, he arrived in Lincoln County bone weary but urgency driving him on. Outside a crowded saloon, Buckshot hitched his lathered mount and headed inside for a hot meal and any whispers that might point him toward Billy. The contents of the letter had weighed on him mightily during the long ride. What brutal harm was that mad dog unleashing now?

Billy had grown up rough, orphaned young when his mother died of tuberculosis in a filthy tenement. He never knew a father. Shuffled through foster homes, Billy became a cunning escape artist eluding whatever confinement was placed on him. By his teens, he had fallen in with a band of thieves and soon outpaced them all in audacity. What he lacked in stature he made up for with boldness and speed with a gun. He felt no loyalty beyond himself, changing sides and allegiances on a whim if it suited him. The Lincoln County range war had cemented his reputation as a gunfighter to be reckoned with. But to Buckshot, he would always be that cocky kid too full of himself.

Digging into a hot meal at a corner table beneath a flickering lantern, Buckshot kept one ear cocked for any talk at the other tables. Finally he picked up on nervous murmurs from nearby ranchers discussing recent raids on their stock. Cattle and horses had been rustled in the night by a growing band of outlaws the last weeks. It sounded like Billy was back to his old ways, and Buckshot's path was clear. He would track the gang to their hideout and finish this for good.

Approaching the ranchers casually after they finished eating, Buckshot inquired about their recent troubles. They were wary at first of this rugged stranger prodding into their business. But noting the shining Sheriff's star on his coat, the ranchers opened up with details of where the gang had hit each homestead and the directions they had disappeared with the stolen stock. Piece by piece, Buckshot formed a map in his head of where their bolt hole must be located. North of town, up in the high rock canyons away from prying eyes. He'd find them there, no doubt. Promising the ranchers he aimed to end the plundering for good, Buckshot secured a fresh mount and headed out alone into the wilderness.

The terrain grew more rugged and inhospitable the further he tracked up into the mountains. Sheer rock walls towered to either side of the twisting canyon passage. An wrong turn here could mean disaster, but Buckshot felt sure he was on the right path. The hoofprints told of large numbers of cattle and horses being driven through recently. Billy and his gang were holed up nearby awaiting another big score. But this time justice was coming for them.

Topping a rise, Buckshot spotted thin tendrils of smoke rising ahead from a hidden hollow. Dismounting and tying off his horse securely, he stealthily closed the remaining distance on foot. Bellying up to the cliff edge on his stomach, he silently peered down at the bustling transient camp below. Makeshift structures sprawled through the canyon, crammed with un-kempt, hard-looking men gambling, drinking, fighting. Staked out on a picket line were dozens of cow ponies and finer steeds that could only be stolen goods. The place seethed with lawless energy. And there, right in the middle, seeming to hold court was the man himself – Billy the Kid. He looked more dangerous than ever.

Buckshot eased back from the cliff edge and considered his next move carefully. Though he had faced worse odds before, being one against forty was risky to say the least. But slipping away now would only let the vipers' nest grow. This evil needed cutting out here and today. Buckshot was suddenly glad he had declined Sheriff Brady's offer of a posse for this task. He knew what must be done, and it was his alone to answer for.

Waiting until full dark, Buckshot worked his way slowly down the treacherous canyon wall using the blackness for cover. He silently padded toward the horse picket line, careful not to stir the restless mounts. Choosing quickly, he cut loose six tough-looking roping steers – perfect for what he had planned. Gathering the jittery cattle, he drove them quietly away into the night. Stopping a safe distance from the camp, he settled in to wait as the first hints of dawn lightened the eastern sky.

Right on cue, as the sunlight crept down the canyon walls the lookouts sounded the alarm of the missing cattle. Buckshot heard shouts and curses from the camp as Billy's men scrambled to investigate. Moments later they came whooping over the rise in pursuit of the lost steers. Just as Buckshot expected, Billy himself rode at the head of the chase – he never could resist a hunt. They pounded right past Buckshot's concealed position without noticing him. That suited Buckshot perfectly. Now the real plan was in motion.

Moving swiftly, Buckshot returned to the outlaw camp while most of the gang was distracted chasing the phantom cattle thieves. A few sentries remained behind, but most were sleeping off last night's revels. Buckshot stealthily disabled the two sentries first with blows to the head before they even realized what was happening. That just left the dozen or so hardened criminals scattered amongst the ramshackle huts, hardly innocents. But if his desperate gambit worked, their own lawless ways would be their undoing.

Fanning the campfires with brush to build the flames, Buckshot moved quickly between structures setting them ablaze. The wind whipped the fires hungrily from building to building as cries of alarm arose from those within. Desperate men staggered out, only to be greeted with a bullet to the leg or arm that dropped them moaning but alive. Buckshot worked his way through the camp leaving behind only crippled outlaws and raging fire. From the chaotic ruins he rode away without looking back, his pistol smoking by his side.

Less than a mile distant, Buckshot halted at the edge of a towering cliff overlooking a deep gorge spanned by a rickety rope bridge often used by locals as a shortcut. But the bridge could only support one man and horse at a time. It was the perfect spot to make a stand with the odds evened up some. Dismounting, he cut both support ropes almost through. As expected, within minutes the thunder of approaching hoofbeats signaled Billy and his gang returning from their fruitless cattle chase. Buckshot gripped his pistol and waited.

When Billy came galloping up the trail to find Buckshot blocking his way, the murderous shock on the outlaw's face quickly turned to madness. "How in damnation..." he sputtered before Buckshot's booming words cut him off.

"I warned you to change your ways, Kid. Instead you've done nothing but spread more wickedness." Buckshot stood relaxed but ready atop the small rise, forcing the gang to rein up short. "Your tyranny ends now. Surrender and you'll get a fair trial."

Billy drew himself up furiously in the saddle. "The only justice here will be me decorating these canyon walls with your insides!" he spat. His hand dropped to his holster. "Ride him down boys!"

In a body, the gang charged uphill heedless of the danger ahead, consumed by blind vengeance. Only Billy held back, watching it unfold with malevolent delight.

Calmly standing his ground, Buckshot called out "Here's your first taste of justice boys" as he fired one shot to sever the final bit of rope anchoring the suspension bridge. With a groan of splintering wood, the bridge swung free from its moorings. The lead riders attempting to cross could only scream in terror as they plunged into the abyss along with their mounts. The rest of the gang desperately fought to pull up or throw themselves from their horses before the drop loomed before them. Within seconds, half a dozen men and horses lay dead or dying at the bottom of the gorge. The remainder milled in shock and panic on the far side as they realized the trap that had been laid for them.

Rage overtaking his shock, Billy drew his pistol and fired wildly across the divide at Buckshot. But the distance was too great for accuracy. Buckshot calmly reloaded his spent cartridge and leveled his weapon at the trapped outlaws.

"Still I offer you the chance to face justice proper," Buckshot called over firmly. "Else the rest will join your brothers down there." He aimed meaningfully at the bridge remains dangling behind the gang. The outlaws glanced fearfully between him and the canyon depths, unsure if surrender or the gunslinger was more dangerous now.

Before they could decide, a ball of fury tore out of their midst, galloping upriver. It was Billy making a break for it alone. Rather than waste shots, Buckshot sprang into his own saddle to give chase on the high trail along the canyon rim. Thus began a thundering race between two determined souls, one running from retribution and the other ruthlessly claiming it.

Billy drove his sweat-lathered mount recklessly over the rough terrain trying to lose Buckshot, but he clung doggedly to the trail. They were well-matched as riders, both lightweight and skilled. But Billy's desperation drove him beyond all reason or care. More than once his horse nearly went over the edge when the narrow path crumbled beneath thundering hooves, but Billy cruelly spurred the courageous beast on. There was no crime he would not commit before surrendering this day.

As the sun reached its zenith, Billy realized he could not shake his pursuer. Wheeling suddenly, he drew his pistol and fired directly at Buckshot. But the distance and his unstable perch rendered it fruitless. Holstering his own gun, knowing it useless now, Buckshot simply spurred his tough mustang on faster. Billy may have been wild, but Buckshot and his mount were relentless as the tide.

The final moments came in a flash. Billy turned once more to fire and his horse stumbled on loose rocks. As the animal went down, Billy was thrown forward directly into the path of Buckshot's pounding steed. Unable to stop its momentum, the mustang trampled Billy under thundering hooves. When the cloud of dust cleared, there lay the notorious outlaw broken and motionless. The man who had eluded frontier justice for so long would finally cheat it no more. His wickedness ended here, beneath a silent sky.

Dismounting slowly, Buckshot approached and looked down upon his old foe. Billy's sightless eyes stared upward as if in final surprise at the turn of fate. Reaching gently down, Buckshot drew the fellow's jacket across his battered face. Another violent chapter of the untamed frontier closed in red dirt. Without a word, Buckshot mounted up and headed home to Violet, his duty complete. Billy the Kid would ride the high country in infamy and song, but those who buried loved ones would mourn a time longer. All loose ends were now neatly tied, for good.

The long journey passed more quickly it seemed, now that purpose no longer drove Buckshot on with vengeance in his heart. Violet was waiting joyfully on the porch when he rode weary but content back into Deadwood. That night in the comfort of their own bed, Buckshot told Violet of the task's completion and the peace it had brought him. The next morning, rested and eyes bright again, they spoke optimistically of the future and the life they would continue building together.

Weeks later, Buckshot had returned to the steady rhythms of ranch work and domestic comforts with his wife. But something still nagged at him from the encounter with Billy. A unfairness inherent in how such things unfolded on the frontier, where often the most ruthless and foolhardy grabbed the glory while decent folk lived and died unknown. It stirred Buckshot's old rebelliousness against injustice.

One night by the fire, Violet perched nearby sewing, Buckshot revealed what he aimed to do. "I've been pondering how Billy will likely become immortalized in dime novel legend while the real folk of Lincoln County remain forgotten," he explained. "So I'm minded to tell their true stories in a book – the farmers and lawmen and such who tried building lives there. It's time Billy's myth was dispelled."

Violet smiled knowingly, her needle never pausing. "Your heart has always stood with the humble upright souls whom rogues have wronged," she said approvingly. With her blessing, Buckshot began reaching out to folks who could help him compile the oral histories into a book celebrating not the killers of Lincoln County but the lives and community those villains had shattered. It was a fairer legacy.

The task ended up taking years, as Buckshot sought out aging pioneers scattered throughout the territory one by one to record their experiences in that troubled corner of the untamed frontier. The picture he slowly assembled was of resilient ordinary people – miners, shopkeepers, widows, clergy and more – struggling to build a just and lawful society. Good folks who valued faith, family and fellowship. Not mythic demons or angels, but real heroes all the same for their quiet courage and sacrifice in making that wilderness a place fit for civilization.

At long last the undertaking was complete. With Violet's help publishing the collection of stories from the people of Lincoln County themselves, the book was distributed across the frontier. While Billy the Kid and Pat Garrett would live on in popular culture's imagination, now there would be a truer record for history. Buckshot was glad he could give something back to that community which had suffered so much turmoil. Though long delayed, he hoped it brought their descendants some peace.

In the end it mattered not if Buckshot Roberts's name was recalled in future generations. Fame held no allure for him. But perhaps some good could come from one who had walked in darkness being drawn back into the light. If any echoed his story, let it be not for the blood spilled but the grace found. There was hope, there was redemption. For what is an outlaw but one forgotten the love that binds us all as one? When Buckshot left this world, it was into Violet's embrace eternal, made whole.

Chapter 7 - Preparations for the Big Gunfight

Buckshot arose before sunrise, determined to use every possible moment to prepare for his upcoming showdown with McCreedy. Though he had prevailed in their first confrontation, the outlaw chief would not underestimate him again. Victory would require Buckshot's utmost cunning and skill.

After stoking up the morning fire, he sat quietly contemplating the coming ordeal while strong coffee brewed. So much more than his own fate hung in the balance this day. The future peace of Deadwood depended on Buckshot vanquishing McCreedy once and for all. But doubt and dread roiled beneath his stoic surface.

The creak of floorboards announced Violet rising from their bed. Silently she came and nestled close beside Buckshot, laying her head on his shoulder. No words needed to be said. Her steadfast presence gave Buckshot strength. With a last tender kiss, Violet left to ready herself for the difficult day ahead, never betraying the fear in her eyes. Buckshot's heart swelled at her stalwart courage on his behalf. He could ask no truer partner in this life.

Fortified by coffee and Violet's quiet faith in him, Buckshot prepared for the task at hand. His trusted Colt pistols were cleaned and loaded methodically. Nothing could be left to chance. These six-shooters must not fail him today. Satisfied with their operation, Buckshot lovingly polished the worn grips before sliding the Colts into their well-worn holsters. The familiar weight on his hips fortified his spirit.

Dressing with deliberation, Buckshot chose a simple white linen shirt devoid of frills, along with black trousers and boots. He would meet destiny neatly appointed. His battered hat had weathered many close shaves at his side - it rightfully deserved to top off the ensemble. Attire sorted, Buckshot headed downstairs where Violet had prepared a hearty meal, despite her own anxiety. Bless her for sustaining him this day.

Their conversation over breakfast was subdued but intimate. Hand in hand, they lingered long over the last sip of coffee, putting off the inevitable parting as long as possible. But the hour could not be delayed forever. With trepidation Buckshot helped Violet into her coat and escorted her to the boarding house where the other women of the town would pass the day in fretful waiting. At the porch they embraced desperately, reaching across an unknowable gulf this day had opened between them. Violet's final kiss left a bittersweet tang.

Walking slowly towards destiny alone, Buckshot recalled when their paths had first crossed that fateful day - Violet an oasis of light in the surrounding gritty chaos into which she had wandered. From that unlikely meeting, Buckshot's once aimless course now had meaning and purpose beyond himself. The love they had built shielded his soul and showed the man he truly wanted to be. No matter the cost, their shining dream must endure.

Nearing the center of town, Buckshot saw that full daylight had brought citizens out nervously into the streets. Hopeful gazes followed him. The fate of their community lay squarely on the shoulders of one former wayward gunslinger who had finally chosen the right side. Buckshot stood tall beneath their collective trust - he would not fail them in this dark hour.

Glancing toward the large saloon, Buckshot noted the stallions hitched out front bearing McCreedy's brand. Good - the villain had not fled but seemed determined to face the consequences, same as Buckshot. Perhaps a shred of courage yet beat within the black-hearted outlaw, but it would not save him now. The hour of destiny was nigh.

With a final check of his pistols, Buckshot strode across the dusty street and thrust open the doors into the smoky gloom within. Townsfolk drew back in dread from the doors as shouts sounded from inside. Buckshot's jaw clenched as he stepped forth to meet his fate. Let it be decided here.

No time for drink or nerves - McCreedy's roar of challenge greeted Buckshot the instant he entered. "I've been awaiting ya, hero!" the big outlaw bellowed from the middle of the room, flanked by a dozen of his hard-bitten henchmen. "This town ain't big enough for the both of us!" McCreedy's hands hovered menacingly by his holstered Remington pistols. His men bristled with an array of weaponry, cutthroats to the last. The final showdown between lawman and outlaw was at hand.

Buckshot surveyed the scene, his expression stony. The odds were long, but the room gave space to maneuver and seek cover needed. Tables remained upright, awaiting the bullets soon to embed there. The terrified bartenders and whores hugged the walls, clearing the field of battle. These reluctant spectators knew frontier justice was harsh and unflinching. Not all would stand to toast the victor's victory.

"Your criminality ends here, McCreedy," Buckshot declared, voice echoing in the tense stillness. "Best surrender and spare good lives being cut short." His steely eyes never left McCreedy. He had offered absolution, though they both knew the road ahead now. McCreedy would accept only one way out of this saloon this day - feet first.

The outlaw chief threw back his head and roared malicious laughter. "Ain't you high and mighty for a scoundrel once hunted hisself! But them days are done - you're the one who'll exit boot heels first!" McCreedy's huge pistol cleared its holster in the blink of an eye. "Say howdy to the devil, lawdog!"

In that split second as McCreedy drew down, Buckshot was a blur of motion - his twin Colts leaped into his hands and blazed fire before the echo of McCreedy's threat faded. Buckshot's slug tore through the outlaw's right shoulder in a spray of blood, spinning McCreedy sideways with a scream of pain and fury. His own wild shot went high, shattering a lantern above the bar in a rain of glass and flame. And thus hell erupted within those confined walls not built to contain it.

The rest was chaos incarnate. Both sides drew weapons and the saloon exploded in thunderous gunfire, shot and powder smoke. Whores fled screaming into the street while the bartenders cowered beneath their precious bottles and patrons dove for cover. It was every man for himself in that lead-filled deathtrap. The devils of vengeance and self-preservation unleashed within.

Buckshot rolled behind a heavy table kicked over in the melee as flying lead splintered wood and plaster all around. Kneeling up quickly, he squeezed off four rapid shots from his Colts into the hellish murk before dropping down again to frantically reload.

Across the room McCreedy blazed away one-handed, bellowing curse and command to rally his staggered men. The outlaw meant to fight this out to the bitter end.

Both sides exchanged blistering fusillades, filling the saloon with the crack and tang of pistol fire. Papered walls were shredded, mirror and bottles exploded in glittering shards, furniture demolished in the smoking chaos. Wounded men cried out for mercy or their mothers as they bled lives irredeemable into the sawdust. But neither side dared yield now. The remorseless mathematics of violence ruled the day's final sums.

In the ebb and flow Buckshot at times found himself horrifyingly exposed as the lawless tide surged and receded unpredictably in the choking gun smoke fog. Lunging over the bar to avoid a hail of lead, he slipped on spilled liquor and crashed down amidst the glittering wreckage. Scrambling desperately for cover as boots thundered nearer, his hands closed unexpectedly around two stout liquor bottles somehow unbroken.

Crude weapons in hand, Buckshot peered over the bar's remains to glimpse three of McCreedy's men closing in with bloodlust, pistols leveled for the kill. With no time or room to aim a firearm, Buckshot reared up with a guttural cry and hurled his bottleneck missiles with all his fury. Two pistols cracked simultaneously but the shooters fell back clutching savaged faces as whiskey and glass orbited viciously through the gun smoke. Fortune favors the bold! Seizing the gambit, Buckshot dispatched his staggering foes with point blank shots before more could press the advantage.

For a desperate moment the saloon fell silent but for the groans of the suffering. Buckshot braced for McCreedy's next onslaught. Instead sound of a heavy body collapsing drew all eyes. Through the haze McCreedy could be glimpsed sprawled prone behind an overturned table, his remaining henchmen clustered around him anxiously. Buckshot had almost forgotten the shoulder wound he inflicted at the start. Now fate may have dealt an unexpected card in his favor if the black-hearted outlaw was unfit to fight on.

Sure enough, McCreedy's raging voice could be heard cursing violently as his men restrained him. Buckshot clearly made out the words "get me to the Doc's!" as the hulking outlaw was dragged towards the rear exit. The remaining handful of gang members provided cover fire allowing their leader to retreat, hateful eyes fixed on Buckshot even as they backed away.

As the gunfire died down, silence descended on the devastation. The saloon interior was utterly demolished, blood splashed across the shuddering witnesses. Buckshot stood rigid, smoke wisping from his Colts. McCreedy had been routed, albeit likely only temporarily. But fortune had granted Buckshot this victory in their first clash. As the townsfolk cautiously emerged to survey the carnage, he knew the greater battle was only begun. McCreedy did not accept defeat - he sought only vengeance. And then God help them all.

In the aftermath, Buckshot gave no thought to his own minor cuts and powder burns. His only concern was Violet, so he hurried to the boarding house and up the steps. The moment the door opened to reveal her beloved face, all Buckshot's tension melted away. She flew to his arms and they clung wordlessly together, the best balm for all hurts. Gently Violet tended to his injuries as he recounted the saloon's destruction. Her only response was a fervent "Thank the heavens you survived."

Supper was taken privately in their room. Little was said but much conveyed in each understanding look and touch, reaffirming their unbreakable bond. Later by candle light they lay entwined, speaking softly of an uncertain future. Buckshot confessed his gut certainty McCreedy would return for bloody retribution. Violet murmured sadly that only one of them would leave this town still breathing when that time came. Buckshot could make no promises except that he would face whatever awaited with courage. Violet tenderly kissed each rough knuckle and whispered she had no doubts on that count. Her abiding faith girded Buckshot's spirit for the trials ahead. Holding his beloved close beneath the lonely night sky, he found some brief respite.

Dawn came cruelly as ever. Buckshot rose grimly knowing the day could bring McCreedy's return. His wounds were still fresh but the outlaw's hatred would overcome all pain to see Buckshot dead. Violet clung fiercely at the door, her head tucked against Buckshot's chest and her delicate frame trembling beneath his enfolding arms. He breathed deep the lavender scent of her hair and whispered reassuringly "This too shall pass, my love." Looking up at him with eyes that laid her very soul bare, Violet touched his cheek and simply said "Come back to me." Buckshot kissed her tenderly, then turned to face the day, her love the armor girding his heart.

Nearing the center of town, Buckshot's ears detected an ominous drone that set his nerves on edge before the source came into view down the dusty street. A seething thunder of approaching hoofbeats rumbling like the very hordes of hell on the horizon. heartsick, Buckshot knew vengeance had arrived sooner than expected. Drawing his Colts with grave calm, he strode out to meet his fate as the first riders came into view through the scorching heat shimmers. God stand with the righteous this day.

Chapter 8 - Buckshot Roberts Visits His Sweetheart

The day following Buckshot's bloody confrontation with McCreedy at the saloon, he rose restless and on edge. Though the outlaw boss's injuries had granted Deadwood a reprieve, the coming reckoning still weighed heavy on Buckshot's mind. He yearned to see Violet, needing her soothing presence to quiet the lingering violence churning within him.

After downing some coffee, Buckshot headed out into the cool dawn. Most folks were still shuttered inside, wary of lingering threats. The main street lay empty, with only a stray dog loping down the dusty road. Buckshot's spurs jingled loud in the uneasy quiet as he made his way towards Violet's boarding house.

Ascending the creaky steps, Buckshot gave a soft knock. After a moment, the door opened just a crack to reveal Violet's anxious face peering out. Seeing it was him, her eyes flooded with relief and she quickly ushered Buckshot inside. Violet murmured that she had passed a long and lonely night fraught with worry since they had parted. She clung to him fiercely, as if to reassure herself her beloved was truly still there. Buckshot regretted deeply causing her such distress. He tenderly stroked Violet's loose dark hair, murmuring words of comfort until her trembling ceased.

When she had collected herself somewhat, Violet brewed a strong pot of coffee and prepared a light breakfast from the house's provisions. They ate side by side, speaking little but deriving much solace from each other's presence after the storm of the previous day. By unspoken assent, the impending dangers went unmentioned for now. This moment was theirs alone, a refuge from chaos.

Their repast finished, Buckshot helped Violet with her coat and hat before they ventured out together into the quiet street. Where the day may lead neither knew nor cared. It was enough simply to wander awhile through the rustic town hand in hand, leaving woes behind for a time. Buckshot felt himself fully relaxing for the first time since the clash at the saloon. Violet's very nearness had a restorative effect on his battered spirit.

Ambling aimlessly down a side street, they came across the small white-steepled church on the outskirts of town. Surprising Buckshot, Violet turned and pulled him towards the modest sanctuary. Within the humble chapel, she lead him to a pew, bade him sit, and settled close beside him.

"I know faith is not always your pillar as it is mine," Violet whispered. "But finding peace here together can only help gird us for the trials ahead." Buckshot considered her words and then nodded slowly. Perhaps something profound dwelt in stillness.

They sat side by side in the cool silence within the stone walls. Shafts of light filtered through stained glass in jewel-bright hues, washing over the weary gunslinger and devoted woman locked in quiet communion. For a timeless interval, the outside world with its looming darkness ceased to be.

After a while Buckshot became conscious of Violet regarding him keenly. He turned his weathered face to meet her sparkling eyes. "What thoughts occupy that mind of yours?" he asked with a wry smile.

Violet leaned into him fondly. "Only gratitude for the blessings that brought your path to mine, despite the troubles we came from and those ahead," she answered. "My faith teaches that love is the cord binding all lost souls together. You and I are reminders of that truth."

Her words moved Buckshot deeply, resonating with a half-formed longing in his own soul. "You are a tonic to my spirit, Violet," he told her. "Your wisdom and goodness are beacons lighting my way out from the dark wilderness I have wandered." Violet smiled radiantly and laid her head against his shoulder. A profound peace filled Buckshot, there in the muted light filtered through saints and apostles benignly watching from the windows.

Some time later they emerged back into the bright day, spirits bolstered. Making their way back through town, they found citizens beginning to stir cautiously and open their doors and shops. News of McCreedy's wounds seemed to have spread some relief that the danger had passed for now. Buckshot only wished that were true.

He escorted Violet to the small cafe where she took lunch with other ladies of the town. Their parting was reluctant, but lingering dread still drove Buckshot to make the rounds, checking in with the sheriff and other upright citizens. All reported quiet, with no sign of McCreedy's gang since they had fled the saloon with their injured leader. Though unsettled himself, Buckshot tried projecting confidence that the outlaw threat was past. He knew worrying minds did no good.

Afternoon found the town largely returned to its familiar rhythms. Buckshot occupied himself usefully repairing a porch damaged during the fighting, allowing his hands and mind some peace. But he remained constantly alert for any signs of trouble. Though the devil had been driven out yesterday, evil did not surrender so easily.

Later, as the day's heat began cooling, Buckshot made his way back to the cafe where he had left Violet. He could see her through the window, smiling and chatting amiably with the other ladies. But their talk and laughter reminded Buckshot painfully of the simple domestic happiness that seemed to ever elude his grasp. A pang of remorse pierced him, knowing Violet deserved more than a wayward wanderer courted by death and danger. She had been raised a genteel lady. But it was too late - losing her now would destroy Buckshot entirely.

Violet's face lit up joyfully seeing Buckshot waiting when she emerged onto the porch. Taking her hand, Buckshot was struck anew by her graceful charm so out of place in this rough-hewn land. He resolved to remain vigilant and defeat whatever evil still lurked out there, so Violet could have the secure future she deserved. Her trusting hand in his reawoke Buckshot's courage.

They supped together in Violet's boarding house parlor, but even here Buckshot sensed the unseen threat lurking right outside the fragile bubble of their happiness. Was nowhere safe? Would contentment be wrenched away just as it felt within his callused grasp? Gazing across the table at his beloved's kind eyes, Buckshot felt only more determination to resist the criminal demons trying to shatter this town's hopes. Wherever the next clash lead, he was ready. He would fight for those too innocent to fight for themselves.

Walking Violet to her room later, Buckshot hesitated at the threshold. Their closeness here seemed painfully fragile, as if these walls could not hold at bay the forces poised to tear apart everything decent. But Violet drew him inside swiftly, closing the door firmly to shut out the outside world. In her sheltering embrace, Buckshot's foreboding melted away for precious hours of refuge. No words needed be spoken in the tender darkness. He fell into blissful sleep still enfolded in her soothing scent, her slim body snug against his broad frame.

Dawn came cruel as ever. Buckshot slipped from the rumpled bedclothes so as not to disturb Violet's precious rest. Dressing silently, he gazed down at her lovely features serene in slumber, as if no darkness existed past this room. His heart ached at the prospect of leaving her to face the threats lurking outside alone. But last night's passion had only strengthened his resolve to tame this wild land for the sake of those good souls hoping to build lives here. With a final longing look, Buckshot stepped into the fraught day. Come what may, those under his protection would be spared harm.

A tense quiet greeted Buckshot outside. The street lay empty, most townsfolk still behind locked doors after the violence of recent days. A foreboding instinct told him the calm could not last. Buckshot's spurs rapped loudly in the heavy silence as he stalked toward the saloon ruins, senses sharp for the first sign of trouble. The day already felt charged, like the heavy stillness before a lightning strike. He rolled a cigarette one-handed, scouring his surroundings constantly as he walked. His gut said a storm was gathering. But Buckshot aimed to meet it head-on when it broke.

Chapter 9 - Billy the Kid Gathers His Gang

News of Billy the Kid's return to his outlaw ways after his run-in with Buckshot Roberts soon reached the ears of like-minded rogues far and wide. His fearsome reputation and thirst for vengeance drew the discontented and reckless to gather under his banner once more. Billy's new gang grew rapidly in those remote high country canyons where he plotted his crusade against the lawmen who had dared cross him.

In a narrow box canyon far from prying eyes, Billy set up their lawless encampment. Ragged tents and lean-tos popped up overnight as dozens of unsavory men filtered in. Most were desperate characters with nothing left to lose - would-be gunslingers eager to make names for themselves, ex-cons dreaming of easy spoils to be had, wasted youths running from responsibility. To these outcasts, Billy offered power, riches, and a righteous cause that appealed to their vanity. In truth he cared only for his own fame and agenda, but discontent was the tinder for his coming blaze of anarchy.

During the day, the canyon echoed with noise - cursing and yelling from drunken brawls, hammering as crude structures went up, horses neighing as new recruits arrived. At night, raucous singing and laughter carried on until dawn from around the roaring bonfires. Stories and boasts were exchanged as liquor flowed freely. A festering outpost of chaos had coalesced, hidden for now within the remote peaks. Into this wild gathering strode Billy to welcome the newest arrivals.

Though still boyish in appearance, Billy had grown harder since fleeing the East. His slender frame radiated raw intensity, brown hair tossing above narrowed eyes glinting wildly in the firelight. The Colt on his hip had seen much use. He moved with coiled energy through the mob of followers, clasping hands and clapping shoulders like an old friend to each. But cold calculation lurked always behind Billy's affable façade. Every man here was but a pawn to his schemes.

Late into the nights Billy held court around the largest bonfire, mesmerizing the gathering with his charismatic rhetoric against oppression. He spoke of being hounded without cause by powerful men, unjustly robbed of property and nearly his life. His stirring tales evoked outrage from listeners who felt their own petty grudges justified. Only by banding together could they protect each other and take back what had been stolen, Billy exhorted. The impressionable mob hung on his every word, ready to follow wherever he led them.

When sentiment neared fever pitch, Billy would stand and raise a defiant fist, roaring of unfinished business with those who had wronged him. Cries for vengeance echoed from the liquored-up crowd. The name of Buckshot Roberts was uttered with particular contempt. In their eyes he was no upholder of justice, but the ultimate symbol of hypocrisy and persecution of their kind. How Billy hated that man who had humiliated him! Well, the reckoning was at hand. Buckshot's days were numbered and these fine people before him would ensure justice was served! More furious shouts greeted this vow of retribution. The gang was nearly ready to be unleashed.

To temper his followers' wilder tendencies, Billy enforced discipline at key moments. Disputes over money or women were quickly broken up at gunpoint before blood was spilled needlessly. "Save your fire for the true enemy!" Billy would snarl.

Rations and equipment were distributed by his lieutenants to avoid squabbling. The chaotic mob was molded into an army through threat and reward. Billy showed no mercy to those who stepped seriously out of line by fighting or stealing from the gang itself. Transgressors simply disappeared, never to return. This kept even the most volatile men leery of testing their leader's limits too far. An undercurrent of fear balanced the fanatical loyalty Billy engendered.

By unspoken consent no guns were ever drawn on Billy himself. He had proven lethally adept at use of his own pistol and knife should anyone dare threaten his absolute authority. Stories abounded of Billy shooting men down over petty slights to their faces, then graciously paying for their burial. Despite his easy humor, crossing the volatile young outlaw could have deadly consequences. The safe route was accepting whatever favors or abuse he doled out with equal cheer. His followers may have numbered in the dozens, but in his sly mind they were naught but Billy's personal arsenal to aim at his enemies.

To toughen up his gang and winnow out the weak, Billy drove them hard on dangerous forays. They raided remote homesteads for supplies, rustled cattle and horses from distant ranches, and robbed unwary travelers on the high passes. Those reluctant to get blood on their hands quickly abandoned the gang's brutal employ. Others succumbed to misjudged gunfights or the harsh wilderness itself. But the most ruthless and capable survived and thrived, bonded by hardship andriches. They became a tight-knit crew devoted to their young chieftain unto death. So the gang was hardened into proper instruments for Billy's vengeance.

As summer waned into autumn, cooling temperatures drove the pack down from the mountains towards civilization once again. Billy aimed to increase the pressure by striking ever nearer settlements, sending his infamy ringing throughout the territory like a war drum. The scattered settlers and townsfolk did not know it yet, but they were prey kept ignorant only by Billy's wily preparation. Soon his wrath would be felt far and wide.

On a golden afternoon, Billy assembled his full gang in the canyon to make ready for their first brazen strike on a real town. Weapons were passed out from crates - pistols, rifles, knives, and ammunition. The mounted men bristled with deadly implements. This raid would be bloody, for Billy was done with restraint. Tonight his vengeance would announce itself openly!

In a great thunder of hoofbeats, the forty-strong war party surged from their hidden canyon lair riding hard for the nearby township of Fort Sumner. They sang and whooped wildly, firing gleefully into the air through the crisp autumn twilight. Solid citizens closed themselves in tightly, dreading what such wanton violence presaged. This night the name Billy the Kid would roar back to terrible life in a hail of lead and smoke. Buckshot Roberts had best be ready, for a storm was hurtling his direction at last!

Billy's bloody return to notoriety in Fort Sumner was but the first falling domino. In the weeks that followed, his gang launched ever more brazen attacks like wolves descending upon isolated sheep. Homesteads were left burning across the territory as gunfire and panic spread. Posses that dared pursue soon lost Billy's savage crew in the trackless mountains they knew so well. None could stand against the tide of terror and lawlessness.

As reward, Billy's legend grew. Fresh recruits arrived daily at the secret canyon camp. Unattached gunslingers eagerly petitioned to join the gang with its rising fame. Even a few Indians sick of the white man's encroachment offered their wilderness skills. An unspoken truce was struck between Billy's gringo gang and these unlikely native allies. All were united in striking back against civilization's chains, no matter their past quarrels.

Surrounded by dozens of armed warriors eager for leadership against the lawmen and judges attempting to corral their freedom, Billy's confidence swelled. His ego was greatly fueled as well by admiring female admirers who left comfort behind to follow this daring outlaw, heedless of the peril. They gazed at him adoringly around the campfires, competing ruthlessly for his fickle affections. Billy enjoyed them thoroughly, then discarded these beauties once his interest inevitably wandered.

The rising notoriety of Billy and his marauders put the territory on edge as winter approached. Governor Lew Wallace himself delivered a rousing speech promising to crush these agents of chaos and tyranny, but lawmen remained reluctant to confront the dangerous gang everyone now feared. Billy and his boys reveled in their burgeoning legend amongst the swayed masses who saw them as romantic champions against oppression.

Once the high passes filled with snow, trapping the gang in their remote stronghold till spring thaw, Billy had no choice but to be patient. Daily, fresh tales were told over whisky and hurrahs to keep spirits high - exaggerated yarns of past raids, close scrapes with the law, and dreams of wealth and fame soon to be theirs. Billy himself spoke little. Privately, he focused his imagination fully on coming vengeance. Out there somewhere, Buckshot

Roberts walked free and unpunished. That would change once the snows melted. When the time came, Billy thought of his old rival often as he lay with the Indian chief's lush young daughter, claiming everything he felt was owed him in this life. She was but another conquest along his path to legend. With all his wild forces now arrayed, nothing would deny Billy his rightful and bloody destiny.

On the day the ice at last cracked and the mountain streams began to swell, Billy stirred his restless men to action. The trials of winter were forgotten in their zeal. Gathering weapons and mounts yet again, the gang raced down into greening valleys bellowing eagerly for the bloodletting ahead. None dared stand before them.

As terrified settlers peeked from behind boarded windows, the barbarians thundered through once-peaceful towns with guns blazing wildly into the air. They whooped and pounded each other's backs at this homecoming. The long wait was over - Billy's legion was unleashed again! Now they rode for the place Billy had vowed would feel his wrath worst of all - Deadwood and the man called Buckshot. That reckoning was nigh!

With his experienced lieutenant Tom O'Folliard riding by his side, Billy led his men through the fertile spring landscape. His reputation cleared their path of any lawmen wise enough not to throw their lives away recklessly. After long months cooped up in the mountains, the gang was spoiling for confrontation. All these green valleys would soon feel the stampede headed their direction.

Through territory once orderly but now gripped by dread, the outlaw regiment advanced. None dared stand before the fearsome onslaught. Buckshot Roberts and Deadwood were hundreds of miles distant, but Billy's fury mounted with each day as if he could already taste the coming bloodletting. There would be no mercy this time. The city leaders who had deceived and betrayed him, and the man who had shot him down, all would pay dearly. Billy would ride into legend over their broken bodies and burning homes. At his wild war cry, the gang surged onward savagely.

Chapter 10 - The Day Before the Gunfight

Buckshot woke well before dawn, feeling the weight of destiny upon him. In just 24 hours he would face off against Mc-Creedy again in the streets of Deadwood. The showdown would decide not only Buckshot's fate, but that of Violet and all the decent citizens hoping to build a just life here. Failure was not an option.

After stoking up the fire against the chill, Buckshot sat quietly sipping bitter black coffee. He tried to let his racing thoughts subside, knowing calm focus would serve him better this day than fretting. There were practical matters yet to be settled before tomorrow's clash. With grim resolution, Buckshot began his preparations.

First he cleaned and oiled his twin Colt pistols with meticulous care until each revolved smoothly and locks clicked crisply. These well-worn companions might be called upon for the finest service of their careers come tomorrow's draw. Satisfied they were ready, Buckshot loaded each empty chamber then spun the cylinders, listening to the deadly music of lead bullets settling into place. The guns were stowed neatly beside his bed before Buckshot headed out to confront the fraught day.

Emerging onto the still-empty street, Buckshot observed the townsfolk's doors remained barred. Fear of McCreedy's return permeated everything. Buckshot's spurs rang loud in the tense quiet as he made his way through the dusty street. He saw the drapes in Violet's boarding house windows stir as she watched him pass by. Pausing, he swept off his hat and bowed slightly to indicate all was well. The curtains stilled again. Heartened knowing Violet kept watch over him, Buckshot continued on.

Arriving at the livery stable, Buckshot was greeted by the musty animal smells of security. His tough roping horse nickered softly in recognition of an old friend. After providing fresh feed and water, Buckshot lifted each hoof in turn, inspecting their condition closely and digging out any stones lodged in the frog. He curried the horse's bay coat until it gleamed. "Big day tomorrow, my friend," Buckshot murmured. The horse bobbed its head as if it understood.

Leaving the livery, Buckshot headed for the small cafe where he could break his fast. The owner was reluctant to open up, but acquiesced after Buckshot swore on his life no trouble would visit these parts today. She served him eggs, bacon and coffee at an outdoor table before retreating warily back inside. Buckshot ate slowly, deep in thought. Every detail must be considered for the coming showdown. When he finished eating, Buckshot made one more stop.

At the town's small church, Buckshot removed his hat and entered quietly. He dipped fingers in the font of holy water near the door, crossing himself in the Catholic fashion of his youth. Slipping into a rear pew, he sat gazing up at the stained glass, considering the presence of powers beyond his own meager abilities. Bowing his head, Buckshot prayed simply for the courage to stand resolute and the wisdom to end this without further bloodshed. He remained there some time in contemplative silence until the padre entered and came over to greet him kindly. They spoke together of duty, justice and forbearance. Leaving the church, Buckshot felt renewed moral vigor - come what may, he would comport himself honorably.

Wandering the town, Buckshot now found himself observing trivial details that suddenly seemed meaningful - children's toys abandoned in yards, a rough bench where he had once sat chatting with Violet, the porch steps where he had finally worked up the nerve to ask her to dinner. Deadwood had become home, although Buckshot had not realized it till faced with the threat to this newfound stability. McCreedy sought to burn it all down. That could not stand.

By now midday had arrived and the relentless sun beat down from its zenith. Buckshot passed the saloon ruins that had hosted the first fateful clash with McCreedy weeks ago. He noted the sheriff's office stood empty still - the lawman was no doubt fortifying his own courage liquidly elsewhere. It would fall on Buckshot's shoulders alone to settle affairs tomorrow. So be it.

As the afternoon's long shadows slowly stretched out, he made his way to Violet's boarding house porch. The lady of the house welcomed him kindly and went to fetch Violet. When his beloved appeared, Buckshot could see she had been crying. Silently he enfolded her into his strong arms. They sat together swaying gently on the porch swing, no words needed. Dreading their parting this night, Buckshot held her until the last possible moment before standing reluctantly. "Until tomorrow, my love," he whispered before pressing his lips fervently to her delicate fingers. Violet mutely clutched his hand in both of hers until distance broke their contact. Buckshot walked on alone under the darkening sky, satisfied he had made peace however fate played out come the morning.

Later, behind closed doors Buckshot inspected his pistol yet again by lamp light, then laid out his clothing for the solemn occasion - white linen shirt, black trousers and jacket, with polished boots and his father's silver spur rowels. The battered hat had been present at his side for so many trials, it deserved a place of honor. If Death's cold hand was his companion tomorrow, Buckshot aimed to meet it dressed proud. With calm purpose he penned a last letter to Violet, then slept untroubled by doubt. At dawn, he was ready.

The morning's stillness felt heavy as Buckshot rose and washed before dressing with care. He fastened each pearl button and straightened the seams with finality. With gun belt affixed and pistols resting easy on his hips, hat topping all, he was prepared to face this good day. A knock at the door heralded the nervous hotel owner come to ask if a last hot meal was wanted. Buckshot assured the man all was well and his kind services would not be needed further. He left a generous payment to cover his stay. thus unencumbered by any worldly affairs, Buckshot stepped forth to seek his destiny this fateful day.

Arriving on the abandoned-feeling street, a folded piece of paper marked with Violet's hand was presented to Buckshot by a shy young girl. "Miss Violet sends this, sir, and says to keep your heart high," she squeaked before dashing off. Unfolding it, he found a short poetic verse Violet had copied -

'Right is on our side - Calm soul, clear eye! Though they seem to die, Wrong shall not prevail! Truth is mightier still, Wrong shall be unreal; Good shall be ideal. Love must sure prevail!'

Reading her final words of faith in him, Buckshot felt profoundly centered. He had left her a letter, but true to her spirit Violet sent inspiration rather than farewell. She was correct of course - righteousness must win out. Though his task today was daunting, Buckshot felt only clarity of purpose. Some foes can be defeated only by refusing to yield to their level. He headed for the town center calm and unbowed. Whatever came, he was ready.

The street remained empty, shutters barred all around. But the citizens were watching, that he knew. As the sun crept higher, Buckshot stood tall beneath its searing rays. A figure appeared from the far end of the lane. McCreedy had arrived, exactly on time. And thus it began, a final showdown inevitable as the turning of the Earth itself. Two steadfast wills locked in mortal combat on behalf of principles bigger than themselves. But only one would walk away when the gunsmoke cleared. All creation seemed to hold its breath.

Chapter 11 - Buckshot Roberts's Last Night in Town

The sun sank low behind the hills surrounding Deadwood, bathing the dusty street where Buckshot stood in vivid orange light. Though the day had been quiet, tension hung over the town like electricity in the air before a storm. All waited tensely for McCreedy's promised vengeance.

Buckshot had faced down the threat unflinchingly, solid as bedrock through which no stream could cut a new path. But standing alone between innocents and chaos exacted a toll. As he rolled a cigarette with callused fingers, Buckshot surveyed the street but saw only the past days flashing like sun sparks on water. Each confrontation seemed to nick away at his weary soul. How much was left to give?

Turning his back on the lengthening shadows, Buckshot set off towards Violet's boarding house and sanctuary. The courage which sustained him against outlaws came from a place beyond his individual strength. He must renew again at that sacred source.

Violet was solemn when she answered his discreet knock, but her face melted into profound relief and love at the sight of Buckshot unharmed. Ushering him in, she shut out the lurking darkness beyond. Here, they created their own small world of light where no evil could intrude.

They shared a modest supper, speaking of simple comforts that strengthened the spirit. Music, poetry, children's laughter, trees budding with new life - these glimmers made the surrounding troubles seem transitory as clouds crossing the sun. Buckshot confessed weariness of spirit to Violet, who listened with kind eyes free of judgment. Her wisdom saw beyond each day's trials to some purpose unfurling gently as a rose's petals.

"My love, you carry a heavy burden not meant for any one soul alone," Violet soothed, taking Buckshot's rough hands in her own delicate grasp. "But no matter what comes, stay true to yourself and we build the foundation to weather any storm together." Her quiet strength bore him up. No further words were needed.

Later, Violet played a soft melody on her grandmother's piano brought west at such difficulty. The notes cascaded gently through the dim room like a spring shower. Buckshot lounged with eyes closed, letting go the coiled tension of the day. Here there was only this hallowed peace shared by two souls that beat as one. For a few hours, the outside world did not exist.

All too soon the lateness of the hour could not be ignored. Every tick of the brass clock nudged them closer to separation and uncertainty. Buckshot's eyes found Violet's, saw there the same dread of this parting. The words that must be said hung silently between them like a blade poised to sever their entwined hearts.

Violet turned away, cheeks wet with tears too proud to fully fall. Gently turning her lace-trimmed chin back to meet his somber gaze, Buckshot spoke fervently. "You are my compass star guiding me through the darkest night. Our love will ever be my sacred shelter, come what may." Eyes glistening, Violet laid her head against his chest and nodded, no other reply needed.

Buckshot stepped reluctantly to the door where each imagined tomorrow waited unseen. There, he enfolded his beloved into one final embrace, feeling her familiar curves yield against him. Violet's lips clung desperately to his, bridging the widening distance between them. Then the door shut with mute finality, leaving him in the cold hallway where duty and destiny called with pitiless urgency.

Outside the night breeze carried notes of music and laughter from the saloon down the street. Buckshot turned his feet there almost unconsciously, wishing to avoid the emptiness of his rented quarters above the livery stable. There at least he would find light and comradeship tonight to hold the lurking darkness at bay.

Hard-bitten cowpokes and soiled doves filled the cramped space. Buckshot eased onto a stool in the back, nodding to those who raised drinks in his direction. "Here's to Buckshot, who's faced down them varmints whilst we was all a-cowering!" declared one grizzled rancher tipsily. "I'll drink to that," Buckshot replied with a wan smile, and threw back the harsh rotgut liquor they pressed on him. He had not come for flattery, but accepting their gratefulness seemed to bolster the weary townsfolk's courage. They would need all of it soon.

As the hours passed, a few of the more sober men drew Buckshot into low conversation. They knew better than most what faced their little settlement come tomorrow's expected onslaught. Every able man was needed to defend what they had built. Grimly Buckshot agreed to provide expert guidance if the worst unfolded. Even those who survived would never reclaim their innocence after the crucible ahead. But at least they would stand or fall as men, protecting kith and kin. Hard times required hard choices. Together they drank to camaraderie in adversity.

The night wore on as ashes crumbled and guttered candles were replaced in the murky room. Buckshot remained alert, ever watching for the tiniest sign of lurking threat. None came, yet still each sudden noise or stumbling drunkard set his nerves on edge. Conflict churned relentlessly in his spirit - dread of what tomorrow might bring warring with determination to face down that old devil once again.

Chapter 12 - Billy the Kid Sets a Trap

The day after escaping the deadly standoff with Buckshot Roberts, Billy the Kid rode as if the devil himself was on his heels. His shoulder throbbed hotly where Buckshot's bullet had grazed him, but even worse was the battered pride. He had grossly underestimated that gunslinger, and it nearly cost Billy his life. Never again - the time had come to end this feud for good.

Reunited with his scattered gang outside of Deadwood, Billy quickly devised a scheme for vengeance. Rather than ride directly back to their hidden canyon base, he led the men on a meandering path designed to confuse any pursuers. Only when certain they had not been followed did Billy finally return to the lawless sanctuary where he reigned supreme.

Back among his motley followers, Billy concealed his simmering rage beneath a jovial façade. He laughed and joked while recounting the confrontation in exaggerated fashion, making it sound as if he had emerged unscathed from toying with his foe. The gullible gang members ate up this version eagerly. Billy's reputation was preserved.

With his wounded shoulder hastily bandaged, Billy joined the gang around the fire for their usual nightly whiskey and tall tales. As was his way, Billy bided his time quietly, speaking little but missing nothing. He studied each man closely, gauging who could be trusted for the delicate task ahead. Patience was key now - he must not tip his hand too soon.

In the following days Billy deliberately kept the gang occupied on routine raids targeting isolated homesteads. They rode far and wide harassing the countryside to vent frustrations and reaffirm their dominance after the humiliation at Deadwood. It would not do to have restlessness and doubt take root in the men's minds. Billy must keep them teetering between wild freedom and his own tight control.

Always, though, Billy's thoughts returned to the true thorn in his side - Buckshot. That stoic lawman had gotten in his head and needed removing, permanently. Billy knew exactly the bait required to lure his calculating foe out vulnerable and exposed. He need only bid his time, constantly watching for the right opportunity among the unwitting followers at his command. Subtle manipulation was a skill Billy had honed young out of necessity.

One evening, as the gang lounged around the latest campfire, Billy noticed a young Mexican member named Jose sitting apart. He was slender with fine features, not cut from the usual outlaw cloth. Billy sauntered over and offered the sullen youth a cigarette. "You seem darker than a preacher's socks tonight, amigo," Billy said lightly. "What weighs on your mind?"

After hesitating, Jose opened up about problems with a local muchacha he was sweet on. Their families were locked in a feud over water rights for their ranches. With prompting from Billy, Jose revealed he had tried persuading the fiercely prideful girl to run away with him, but she refused to abandon her kin as a traitor. Billy made sympathetic noises while memorizing every useful detail for later. Soon he had José cheered up and returned to the fold. But the seed of an idea was already growing in Billy's devious mind.

Several days later, Billy announced to the gang they were riding for the Texas Panhandle. "Plenty of fat slow cattle for the taking down there, boys!" he declared with a flourish. The men whooped eagerly, ready for fresh plunder. Billy had carefully planted hints that law enforcement was scarce in the isolated ranching country they approached. It was the perfect bait.

After long hard days driving the cattle herd north towards their hidden canyon sanctuary, the gang's guard was down. They were not expecting the dozen Texas Rangers who suddenly descended on their camp in the predawn hours, guns drawn. "Drop your weapons!" barked the grizzled captain. "By order of Judge Roy Bean you varmints are under arrest for theft and rustling!"

Stunned, most of the gang surrendered immediately to the infamous Rangers. But Billy was already fleeing on swift bare feet for the treeline. "Let's go boys!" he shouted, spurring the faster men to follow. Gunfire crackled after them from the Ranger's rifles but soon faded as they disappeared into the thickly wooded mesa lands.

By the time the sun crested the horizon, Billy had eluded immediate capture and reunited with those loyal few who had slipped the Rangers' grasp along with him. But now they were the pursued rather than the pursuers, with no refuge but the distant mountain hideout hundreds of miles north. Even clever Billy was shaken by this surprise rout and the long odds now facing them.

It was in that panicked moment that Billy seized upon the desperate opportunity fate had handed him. Calming Jose with a hand on his shoulder, Billy spoke urgently. "Listen friend, we're in a bad fix here. But I know a place we can lay low if we can just get there. That girl awaits." Billy stared intensely into the other young man's eyes. "Will you ride ahead and tell her I'm sending you to fetch her at last? Explain the trouble following us." Jose readily agreed to persuade his sweetheart one last time, gripped by Billy's feigned sincerity.

As Jose raced off toward his family ranch, Billy gathered the remaining men with an ominous tone. "Betrayed!" he rasped harshly. "The Rangers must have gotten word of our camp from a turncoat. Jose has just shown his true colors." Billy paused as if just realizing. "And I know who he's gone to fetch - that girl he's always mooning over! She must be the informant." Angry mutters ran through the men at this revelation. "So here's the play..." Billy continued, laying out a nefarious scheme. Trusted followers would shadow Jose and once the girl emerged, seize them both for harsh interrogation back at the canyon. If his hunch proved correct, Billy might finally gain the leverage needed to finish off Buckshot for good!

Two days later, the party of three gang members Billy had entrusted with the plan returned grimly to the hidden canyon with two prisoners - Jose and the kicking, screaming Mexican girl Billy recognized from description. Now came the true test. As Jose protested their innocence, Billy had the girl separated and dragged to his tent. He emerged hours later looking greatly satisfied. The deed was done - his elaborate fiction was now convincing truth to her ears. Billy ordered Jose restrained for his apparent betrayal, ignoring his former friend's anguished protests. With the stoic old Comanche chief Gray Owl guarding the captives, the rest of the gang melted away to celebrate their leader's cunning triumph.

Late that night, Billy slipped from his tent and covertly freed young Jose, pressing a small bag of coins into his hand. "Here friend, sorry it came to this," Billy whispered conspiratorially. "I don't blame you for sticking by your gal. Get her free and forget this life." The confused young man had no choice but to trust the leader who had always watched his back, and do as directed. Mounting up on one of the gang's fastest horses with the girl seated behind him, Jose quickly fled into the night.

At dawn, the remaining gang members were roused by Gray Owl shouting angrily in Comanche - the two captives were gone! Billy burst from his tent firing his pistol furiously into the air. "Jose has betrayed us again!" he bellowed. "That snake's done snatched his girl and lit out while we slept!" The men milled angrily at this outrage. "But we'll track 'em down," Billy continued darkly. "I wager they'll run straight to the only place he thinks is safe - Deadwood, and that backstabber Buckshot Roberts." The showdown was finally at hand.

By the afternoon, Billy and his gang were riding hard on the trail of the fugitives. In truth, Billy did not care if Jose and the girl lived or died - they were merely bait to lure his true prey. After long months of humiliation, Billy would finally kill the legendary Buckshot Roberts and satiate his burning

Chapter 13 - The Gunfight Begins

As the first rays of dawn light crept over the horizon, the stillness hanging over Deadwood seemed to intensify in anticipation of the confrontation ahead. Buckshot stood alone in the middle of the dusty main street, facing down from afar the silhouette of McCreedy as he emerged from the saloon. The outlaw had arrived, right on time. This fateful day had come at last.

With a cold smile, McCreedy sauntered forward, hand poised arrogantly near his holstered Colt. "Didn't think you'd have the spine to face me again after that licking I gave you last time," he called out mockingly. His men emerged behind him, fanning out with weapons draw. "But if you're so set on dying, I'll grant your wish!" McCreedy raised his hand, signaling his gang to draw down on Buckshot.

Like lightning, Buckshot's pistols were in his hands. His first two shots splintered the stock of the rifles leveled at him before a single finger could squeeze the triggers. The stunned gang members dropped their disabled weapons in the dirt. But McCreedy only snarled, whipping his Colt up to return fire.

The street exploded in thunderous gunfire as both men drew down on each other with deadly speed. Buckshot felt a slug tear through his sleeve, leaving a hot graze on his forearm. His own bullet whistled past McCreedy's head, coming so close it pierced the brim of the outlaw's hat. For an instant they stared at each other down gun barrels wreathed in acrid powder smoke. The final battle had begun.

Diving to cover behind piles of planks and farm tools in front of the livery stable, Buckshot barely avoided the barrage from McCreedy's enraged gang. Furious at his two men being disarmed so quickly, McCreedy had sicced his entire posse on Buckshot. Air whistled with lead as they blasted away with rifles and pistols. The hellish noise was punctuated by awful screams when fighters on either side took mortal lead. The once-peaceful street was transformed into a nightmare.

When his twin Colts ran empty, Buckshot reloaded on the run behind the moving curtain of flying splinters and dust kicked up by bullet strikes near his heels. McCreedy's men tried flanking through the alley but Buckshot cut them down with lethal accuracy even on the move. He tore one rifle from their grasp and used it as a club, ignoring the pain as a bullet grazed his thigh in the melee. There could be no retreat - he must not yield one inch of ground to these demons. Lives depended on Buckshot holding his own here.

McCreedy observed the spectacle with mounting fury as Buckshot continued dodging back and forth in the road, more than a match for the ten hardened outlaws. "That's it!" McCreedy finally roared. "Burn this place to the ground and smoke him out!" At his order, several gang members pulled flasks of whiskey from their dusters and began splashing the potent liquor over walls and porches. As they went to light matches, Buckshot realized the outlaws meant to sacrifice the entire town just to kill him.

Summoning the last of his strength and focus, Buckshot sprang from cover and charged the arsonists before they could ignite the fires. His headlong rush caught them off guard for crucial seconds. Two shots struck home, shattering whiskey bottles and splattering their contents across the dusty ground. A third shot blasted the matches from an outlaw's raised hand just before he could trigger the conflagration. Another gang member went down hard with Buckshot's shoulder slamming into his chest as the gunslinger crashed into their midst. Close by the saloon, chaos reigned as pistols flashed, knives slashed, and men fell.

Having disrupted the incendiaries, Buckshot dived behind the solid oak bar of the saloon porch, gasping for air. He was exhausted and bleeding, but the town still stood. As his vision began to blur, Buckshot feared he had nothing left. The remaining gang members approached slowly, realizing their quarry was cornered and nearly finished. They said nothing but their eyes burned with hate. Buckshot sat slumped in defeat and despair. He had failed.

Suddenly, shouts and pounding hooves heralded a dozen fresh riders galloping up Main Street to surround McCreedy's dwindling force. It was the sheriff and a posse of townsmen! They had seen the smoke and carnage from afar and come prepared for battle. With fury and courage kindled by seeing the damage already wrought, the posse opened fire on the shocked outlaws.

Staggering to his feet, Buckshot peered around the corner of the saloon porch. Blessed salvation had arrived to carry on the fight! He glimpsed McCreedy fleeing into a nearby barn amidst the chaos as the rest of his gang scrambled in all directions. They were breaking at last! Still clutching one of his gore-streaked pistols, Buckshot staggered out and began firing methodically at the gang members fleeing up alleys or taking to horseback. His legs nearly buckled with each step but he refused to quit until the last outlaw was driven off or dead.

As the smoke finally cleared, an eerie silence descended upon the ravaged street now scattered with bodies and discarded weapons. Only the moans of the wounded could be heard. Buckshot sank to his knees, barely conscious. As if in a dream, he saw the sheriff and townsmen rushing up to kneel beside him. "Buckshot! By God, man, you done stood them demons off nearly singlehanded. We arrived just in time," the sheriff said, gripping his shoulder. The brave citizens he had defended pressed in around him, eyes shining with gratitude and awe. Their words of praise swirled meaninglessly around Buckshot as oblivion rose up to claim him. He had kept faith unto the end, but could now rest as darkness took him gently in its arms.

Consciousness returned slowly, accompanied by throbbing pain. Buckshot awoke to find himself propped in bed back at the boarding house. A kindly older woman in a bonnet was pressing a cool cloth to his head while Violet clutched his hand tightly. At the sight of his stirring, Violet let out a joyful sob. "My love, I thought we had lost you!" she exclaimed, showering his haggard face with teary kisses. Her sweet scent and nearness revived Buckshot's spent spirit. With effort, he spoke in a ragged voice, "It'll...take more than that to finish me off." Though his wrecked body screamed otherwise, Buckshot forced a tired grin.

Over the next days, Buckshot drifted in and out restlessly as the fever took hold. His wounds had turned septic, the doctor said gravely. Violet refused to surrender hope, tending Buckshot tirelessly through the long nights, bathing his brow, changing his dressings, willing him to live. The boarding house owner brought broths and potions to force down Buckshot's throat when he awoke briefly delirious.

Finally the fever broke on the third night. Buckshot awoke clear-headed for the first time since the battle, feeling Violet sleeping with her head cradled on his chest. Relief that she was still with him brought tears to Buckshot's eyes. He had been spared to see his beloved's sweet face again. Gently caressing her hair, he let restful sleep reclaim him. The long road back beckoned, but life and light had won out over the forces of darkness.

In the weeks that followed, Violet nurtured Buckshot slowly back to health with her caring ministrations as the town returned to relative peace. The posse had pursued McCreedy's scattered gang far from Deadwood after the fight. Only the wounded remnants had escaped that dreadful day.

Once able to rise from bed and hobble outside, Buckshot was greeted exuberantly by the townsfolk, who considered him their savior against the outlaw onslaught. Buckshot brushed off talk of courage and single-handedly holding off an army of demons. "I just did what needed doing is all," he demurred gruffly. In truth, he was touched by their simple gratitude for standing up when they needed someone to believe in. Buckshot found himself feeling more at home here than anywhere he could recall in his long wandering years.

With Violet's arm supporting him on evening walks, Buckshot gained strength daily as autumnbloomed golden around Deadwood. The future ahead seemed bright with hope instead of darkened by dread. He had faced down his demons without flinching, and found new purpose. McCreedy and his ilk were still out there, but the town had spirit and grit now to handle future threats alongside their guardian gunslinger.

Sitting together on their favorite porch swing, Buckshot pulled Violet tenderly close as crickets chirped in the gathering dusk. "You brought me back in every way that matters," he told her sincerely, calloused hand caressing her delicate cheek. "I'll not leave you lonely again." Smiling through glad tears, Violet nestled into his shoulder. They had weathered the storm and emerged stronger, with deep roots twined together. Come what may, they would stand firm and true till the very end. Buckshot kissed his beloved softly, finally at peace. Whatever path lay ahead, they would walk it together from here on.

Chapter 14 - Buckshot Roberts Gets Hit

The morning sun beat down relentlessly on the bloodstained street where Buckshot faced off against McCreedy and his gang.

Though Buckshot had initially had the upper hand, taking out two gang members quickly, McCreedy soon gained the advantage through sheer force of numbers. With a dozen outlaws blazing away, Buckshot found himself pinned down behind a pile of planks in front of the livery stable. Splintered wood flew as bullets slammed all around him. He was trapped.

Reloading his twin Colts, Buckshot watched for any lull that might allow him to break cover. But McCreedy's men had him surrounded. Whenever he tried leaning out to return fire, a barrage of lead sent Buckshot ducking back down. It was only a matter of time before one found its mark.

Realizing his predicament, Buckshot desperately eyed the wagon parked nearby. If he could reach it, there might be a chance. Taking a deep breath, Buckshot suddenly burst from concealment and sprinted for the wagon, pistols blazing. Caught off guard, two gang members went down clutching bullet wounds. But the rest quickly opened up on Buckshot as he dove behind the wagon's solid oak boards. Their bullets thunked into the thick wood as he scrambled into the dusty hollow beneath the wagon, seeking precious seconds to reload his spent revolvers.

From the darkness, Buckshot heard footsteps approaching. McCreedy's men were advancing to finish him! With no time to reload properly, Buckshot shoved loose bullets directly into his guns' cylinders, then flipped them shut. It was reckless - the cartridges could explode in his hands when fired. But fortune favored the bold. As soon as boots appeared around the wagon's edge, Buckshot thrust both Colts out and pulled the triggers. The outlaws fell back, howling in pain from the dual blasts.

Scrambling out the far side of the wagon, Buckshot broke cover and sprinted towards the saloon where he might find better shelter indoors. Gunshots crackled at his heels as McCreedy's men swung their aim towards him. Leaping over a hitching post, Buckshot made it onto the sidewalk. Just a few more strides now!

Suddenly a sledgehammer slug punched Buckshot's right shoulder, sending him sprawling face first in the dirt. Searing waves of agony told him he'd been hit bad. Gritting his teeth, he clawed his way behind the solid posts supporting the saloon's porch roof. There at least he had cover as he tried to catch his breath against the pain. Buckshot could feel hot blood soaking through his shirt beneath his clutching fingers. The wound was serious, impairing his gun hand. He was in desperate straits now.

Rifles cracked and bullets buzzed past the porch posts shielding Buckshot. It wouldn't be long before the gang maneuvered to draw a bead on his protected position. Bleeding and weakened, with only one good arm left, Buckshot could not realistically fight them off much longer. This seemed his final refuge as the end drew inexorably nearer.

Through the smoke-filled din, Buckshot heard McCreedy shout, "Flank him, boys! We got this trapped rat right where we want him!" Rough voices whooped in anticipation of the kill. They knew Buckshot's time was running out fast. He clutched his remaining pistol tightly, determined to take down a few more before the inevitable end.

As the stomp of boots approached, Buckshot steadied himself, trying to ignore the waves of pain from his ravaged shoulder. He likely had only seconds to take a few desperate shots at the gang closing in for the coup de grâce. This was it - his last stand. Farewell, my love, he thought achingly, picturing Violet's sweet face.

With a wild rebel yell, Buckshot sprang from concealment, lone pistol blazing defiantly at the outlaws rushing him across the debris-strewn street. His shots dropped two, but the rest came on undeterred. As their return fire streaked towards him, everything seemed to slow down. Buckshot realized in that endless split-second that it was over. He had fought to the very end. As he fell, there was no fear or regret, only calm acceptance. His spirit remained unbroken. If this was his time, so be it.

But instead of hard-packed earth, it was strong arms that broke Buckshot's collapse. Dazed, he perceived he was being half-carried, half-dragged back behind the solid oak bar fronting the saloon. A gruff voice shouted close to his ear, "I got you, Buck! Hang in there, help's coming!" Through fading vision Buckshot recognized the sheriff's determined face. An angel of mercy if ever there was.

As the sheriff propped him against the saloon wall and fired back at the closing gang members, Buckshot faded out again. His shoulder was numb now except for occasional fiery stabs whenever he moved. He could feel his life slowly ebbing as crimson soaked the floorboards beneath him. This time there would be no escaping his rendezvous with Death. Yet Buckshot felt only profound relief. He had stood his ground against wickedness until the very last iota of strength left him. Now he could let go this burden, knowing he had kept the faith.

Shadowy figures clustered around where Buckshot slumped. He heard voices shout his name, but they seemed to echo from a great distance now. Buckshot allowed the dark waters closing over him to gently draw his flickering spirit down into their depths. A profound tranquility filled him. He was not alone on this final journey - loving arms seemed to enfold him, easing his passage to whatever lay Beyond. With a long sigh, the light faded...

Sudden searing pain slammed Buckshot back into his body. Blinking against harsh lantern light, he perceived a stranger leaning over him, hands pressing deeply into his wound. Buckshot opened his mouth to curse this fresh torture, but only a weak groan emerged.

"There he is! He's still with us!" exclaimed an excited voice. Through blurred vision, Buckshot recognized the town doctor and Violet hovering behind, wringing her hands anxiously. For her sake alone, Buckshot summoned the willpower to remain tethered to this world a little longer, though every fiber of his being cried out for release from the agony. His ordeal was not over yet.

The doctor and several helpers carried Buckshot on a stretcher to Violet's boarding house nearby and laid him on the bed. Though he faded in and out, Buckshot was conscious enough to notice the tear in Violet's eye as she gently stroked his brow. The doctor's voice filtered through the pounding haze as he conferred gravely with Violet. "The bullet tore clean through the meat of his shoulder. I got the bleeding stopped, but it's a miracle he survived this long. All we can do now is wait and pray the fever does not take hold." Violet nodded stoically before returning to sit vigil at Buckshot's bedside, bathing his ashen face with cool water. For her steadfast compassion, he summoned faint words with cracked lips. "Don't...fret none...over me..." Though wracked with pain, Buckshot managed a weak grin for his be-loved before slipping back into oblivion's embrace.

Delirium descended as infection corrupted Buckshot's body over the next days. He thrashed and moaned ceaselessly atop sweat-soaked sheets, lost in vivid fever dreams of being pursued by phantoms, futilely firing empty pistols to hold them at bay. Kindly hands soothed and restrained him through the long nightmare. When at times Buckshot perceived Violet kneeling in prayer or sleeping with her head resting tenderly upon him, lucidity briefly returned. But soon the sinister visions dragged him back down into their infernal depths. How long could a body and soul endure such suffering?

Finally, after what seemed an eternity, Buckshot awoke with a gasp, feeling the fever had broken. Clean night air filled his lungs instead of the stifling miasma of sickness. His shoulder remained bandaged, but the angry red heat was subsiding. And there slumbered his faithful Violet in her chair beside the bed, looking terribly worn but still lovely to Buckshot's eyes.

Gently he reached out to caress her hair. With a start, Violet sat bolt upright, eyes widening in disbelief and joy at seeing Buckshot return to his senses. "My love!" she cried, taking his hand carefully as tears spilled down her drawn cheeks. She had endured the grim vigil night and day, never surrendering hope even when the doctor's grave prognosis provided none. None had shown greater courage or devotion.

Smiling weakly up at his darling Violet, Buckshot spoke in a ragged whisper, "You saved me...your love drew me back." He tenderly pulled her into an embrace, her head nestling beneath his bearded chin. Be it weeks or months ahead confined to this sickbed, with his tenacious soul mate and guardian angel by his side, Buckshot now knew he would recover fully in time. Black despair had been driven back - he would live on to cherish Violet and laugh in the sunlight again. Where true and selfless love abides, hope ever remains.

In the coming weeks, Violet was beside Buckshot every step through convalescence, gently helping him stand, dress, and take his first hobbling steps. Fresh air, good food and rest slowly restored Buckshot's depleted reserves, along with Violet's tireless care. When he was able, they passed many hours together simply reading or talking softly.

The first time Buckshot managed to descend the stairs and make it outside to sit on the sunny porch, he was greeted by a crowd of well-wishers - the sheriff, townsfolk he had defended and even the preacher. Leaning on his cane, Buckshot tried waving off their ardent praise and gratitude. "You all would've done the same were you in my boots," he demurred. But seeing the simple relief and joy his recovery brought helped much to heal Buckshot's own spirit. This place had come to feel like home, he realized, these folk like family. He had found community for the first time since leaving the wilds.

As Buckshot's strength gradually returned over the following weeks, he began taking short evening strolls around town, Violet's arm linked in his for support. The cool autumn air felt refreshing after being confined indoors. And though his injury had weakened Buckshot for a time, it had only strengthened his and Violet's devotion. They had weathered the storm, and emerged closer for it.

Sitting together on their favorite porch swing, Violet nestled into Buckshot's shoulder as crickets chirped in the gathering dusk. His callused hand caressed her delicate cheek as he said sincerely, "You brought me back in every way that matters. I'll not leave you lonely again." Violet smiled through glad tears, kissing him tenderly. Whatever lay ahead, they would walk forward together from here on. Hardship had only refined their love to a tempered steel, unbreakable now by life's fires.

Chapter 15 - Billy the Kid Retreats

Buckshot stood rigid, smoke wisping from the twin Colts in his grip. At his feet sprawled one of McCreedy's men, felled by Buckshot's crack shot before the outlaw could set fire to the town. The surrounding gang members stared in shock at their fallen cohort, halted in their tracks.

In that frozen moment, a thunder of hoofbeats roared up the street behind the gang. There appeared a dozen mounted men wielding rifles and pistols - the sheriff and a hastily assembled posse! "Surrender, villains!" bellowed the sheriff. Caught off guard, the remaining gang members hastily dropped their weapons and put up their hands. Without McCreedy driving them relentlessly on, their will to fight evaporated.

As the posse swooped in to apprehend the gang, Buckshot sagged back against a porch post, barely standing. His strength was utterly spent after the desperate battle, but Deadwood had endured. Justice had arrived, if only by the narrowest margin. Through his exhaustion, Buckshot felt only profound relief.

The sound of spurs approaching roused him from his stupor. It was the sheriff, beaming with exhilaration. "By thunder, Buckshot, you done held off an army of demons nearly single-handed!

We arrived just in time I reckon." He gripped Buckshot's weary shoulder as the other townsmen clustered around, eyes shining with gratitude for his stand against the outlaws. Their words swirled over Buckshot, fading in and out until his legs buckled. Strong arms lowered him gently to the ground as darkness took him.

Consciousness returned slowly, accompanied by throbbing pain. Buckshot awoke to find himself in bed back at Violet's boarding house. She clutched his hand tightly, eyes red from weeping even as fresh tears of joy spilled down her cheeks. "My love, I thought we had lost you!" she exclaimed, showering him with tender kisses. Her sweet nearness revived Buckshot's spent spirit. "It'll...take more than that...to finish me off," he rasped faintly with a tired grin. Though his body screamed otherwise, he forced himself to appear unbeaten before his distraught Violet.

Over subsequent days, fever set in as Buckshot's wounds turned septic. He thrashed in delirium through vivid nightmares of being hunted by phantoms, relentlessly firing empty pistols. Violet remained steadfastly at his side, bathing Buckshot's burning brow and praying over him until the fever finally broke on the third night. Emerging from the hellish illness, Buckshot found Violet slumbering beside him. Gently caressing her hair, his heart swelled with love for this tenacious woman who was his salvation.

In the following weeks, Violet tenderly helped Buckshot stand, dress, and take his first hobbling steps around the room. Fresh air, hearty food and rest slowly restored his strength, along with Violet's tireless care. The first time he made it outside to sit on the sunny porch, Buckshot was greeted by the sheriff, townsfolk he had defended, and even the local preacher. Leaning on his cane, he tried waving off their ardent praise and gratitude. But seeing the simple joy his recovery brought helped heal his battered spirit. This place felt like home now. He had found community.

As Buckshot's vigor returned over time, he and Violet began taking short evening strolls around town, her arm linked in his for support. The cool autumn air felt refreshing after being bed-ridden so long. Though still weakened from his injury, Buckshot grew stronger daily. Hardship had only deepened his and Violet's devotion. Whatever lay ahead, they would now walk forward together.

Meanwhile, the posse had harried the remnants of McCreedy's shattered gang far from Deadwood after the fight. Even the noto-riously fearsome outlaw leader now knew this territory was lost. Avoiding major settlements, the dozen survivors headed north-east into the high mountains. McCreedy seethed with bitterness over his humiliating defeat after coming so close to crushing his nemesis. But with most of his men dead or imprisoned, even he was forced to retreat for now, despite his burning desire for vengeance. The day's battle had cost him dearly.

Roaming ever north and east with the sheriff's posse on their trail, the tattered remnants of the gang backtracked to the lawless mining settlements of the Dakota Territory where McCreedy had first recruited his crew. There they found temporary refuge from pursuit among the transient claim jumpers and prospec-tors. In that rugged country, questions were rarely asked so long as a man worked claims hard and spent free coins freely.

McCreedy wasted little time in resuming his criminal ways, gathering the most hardened and cold-blooded men to fill out the ranks of his diminished gang. With a fresh infusion of gun hands and fierce new lieutenants, he soon felt emboldened to pick up where he had left off. The wild mining camps made rich targets for robbery once the gold shipments started arriving from the deep tunnels. Those camps stewing with rough characters also provided perfect scapegoats when the jobs turned bloody. The chaos of greed and lawlessness suited McCreedy's purposes now.

But once the snows began falling heavy over the high passes into Montana, activity dwindled for the season. McCreedy and his men became snowbound in a mountain settlement called Bear Gulch, biding time until roads cleared in spring. Isolated in the remote mining town, McCreedy's fury festered and grew through the bitter winter months as he obsessively dwelled on how close he had come to crushing Buckshot. He swore that gunslinger would not elude him again once the trails opened up. Come spring, McCreedy would unleash fresh hell upon Deadwood, burning it to cinders if need be. He had unfinished business with Buckshot Roberts, and intended to confront destiny once more.

When at last the mountain snowmelt swelled the streams into roaring rapids, McCreedy rallied his men to ride south before sentiments turned soft and memories blurred over the cold months. "What we started, we're gonna finish!" McCreedy bellowed to the cheering gang. "Ain't no one gonna deny us what's owed!" Though the journey would be long and hard going back down through the Rockies so early in the season,

McCreedy drove his gang ruthlessly onward. He knew Buckshot and Deadwood would never expect a full-fledged assault from the mountains before winter had fully released its grip. The element of surprise would allow McCreedy to descend on his enemies like an avalanche. He aimed to leave only death and ruin in his wake across Deadwood, wiping the very name of that town from memory.

Pushing south through the icy high passes still deep in snow, there were times even McCreedy second-guessed the wisdom of this early trek to vengeance. Several men and horses were lost tumbling into ravines or freezing to death in unrelenting blizzards. Each casualty fueled McCreedy's fury higher against the man who had forced this hardship upon them. Driven by his master's iron will, the battered gang pressed on until finally the passes began to clear and game returned to the forests. When at last they glimpsed grassy valleys unfolding below, the outlaws raised a weary cheer. Their bloody destination lay ahead at last.

In the fresh mountain meadows, they recuperated aching bodies and gorged themselves on elk steaks and trout. McCreedy granted them a few days' rest and refit, knowing he would need his men fit and ready for the bitter fight ahead. Finally the day arrived - saddling up at dawn, McCreedy lead the gang on the final descent out of the Rockies down towards Deadwood, where destiny awaited. As they rode forth, an eagle cried ominously overhead, spiraling high on the thermals rising from the sun-warmed valley. McCreedy took it as an omen in their favor. He would rend Buckshot Roberts's beating heart from his chest and feed it to that majestic bird. Their victory was at hand!

Chapter 16 - Buckshot Roberts's Last Words

The day of reckoning had arrived. Under the searing midday sun, Buckshot Roberts stood alone in the center of Deadwood's dusty main street. At the far end, the ominous silhouette of McCreedy appeared, sauntering forward with hand poised arrogantly near his holstered Colt.

"This town ain't big enough for the both of us," McCreedy growled, venom in his eyes. "Time to send you to boot hill, hero."

Buckshot met his glare unflinchingly. "Your villainy ends here, McCreedy."

With blinding speed, McCreedy drew first, but Buckshot was a split second faster. His bullet tore through McCreedy's gun hand, eliciting a howl of pain and rage. Clutching the mangled hand spouting crimson, McCreedy could only watch in impotent fury as Buckshot spun his smoking Colt casually before re-holstering it.

"Yield, devil," Buckshot commanded. "Stand down and face justice proper."

"Go to hell!" McCreedy spat back. Whistling shrilly, he signaled his gang to open fire on Buckshot.

From windows and rooftops, a dozen outlaws rose up blasting away with pistols and rifles. Caught in the perilous crossfire, Buckshot dove behind a heavy wagon for cover as angry lead shredded the air around him. He returned fire when able, splintering boards and knocking one shooter off his perch with a pained yell. But Buckshot was pinned down badly.

Realizing he couldn't win this fight alone, Buckshot decided to try something desperate. Waiting for a pause in the gunfire, he broke from cover and sprinted towards the largest structure in sight - the saloon. Bullets kicked up dirt on his heels as outlaws swung their aim his way.

Hitting the saloon doors at a full-tilt run, Buckshot crashed into the dim interior, bowling over a pair of stunned card players. He frantically overturned tables to create a barricade then vaulted the bar, landing with a painful thud amidst shattered glassware. From this vantage, Buckshot began blasting away through the windows at any gang member who dared expose himself, driving them back towards cover.

"We got the bastard trapped now, boys!" Buckshot heard Mc-Creedy bellow from outside. "Bust in and smoke him out!"

The saloon windows and doors suddenly erupted in a hurricane of splintering lead as the gang opened fire full force. Bottles shattered and mirrors exploded as bullets filled the confined space. Buckshot kept his head low, crawling through the wreckage as deadly projectiles chewed up the interior around him. He knew his position was hopeless if help didn't arrive soon. Where was the sheriff and the townspeople?

As the saloon rapidly disintegrated around him under the relentless hail of bullets, Buckshot considered making a mad dash for the back exit. But he quickly dismissed the idea as suicide with the gang waiting to cut him down outside. His only viable option was trying to pick off the outlaws one by one from cover and buy time for the cavalry to hopefully arrive. The saloon had become Buckshot's last refuge, and almost certainly his tomb as well.

Loading his final handful of bullets into the twin Colt pistols, Buckshot steadied his breath and nerves. This was it - his final stand. "May your aim be true, old friends," he whispered, caressing the revolvers' smooth grips. Then with a rebel yell, he reared up blazing away through the drifting gunsmoke at the shadowy forms surrounding the saloon. The heavy pistol roared deafeningly in the confined space as lead tore back towards those trying to kill him.

Through the haze, Buckshot glimpsed at least one outlaw spin and fall beneath his barrage. But then his pistols clicked empty. With no time to reload, Buckshot could only hurl them in desperate fury at the nearest shooters visible through the shattered windows. A shrill cry told one found its mark.

Now utterly defenseless, Buckshot slumped back down behind the wrecked bar as hellfire lead tore through the air over his head. There was no hope left - he was finished. A strange peace settled over him. He had fought to the bitter end as best he could, and that was all any man could do. If this was his fate, then so be it.

As muzzle flashes drew closer through the smoking gloom, Buckshot closed his eyes, preferring to meet death unflinching but unseeing. Violet's beautiful, loving face appeared in his mind's eye, and he clung to that image. Then roaring gun blasts shattered the vision, and searing bullets ripped into Buckshot's chest and gut. The impacts slammed him flat onto the floorboards amidst debris and spilled alcohol. Mortally wounded at long last.

Through the ringing in his ears, Buckshot heard footsteps approach slowly until McCreedy's leering face loomed over him, twisted with vengeance fulfilled. The cold press of a pistol barrel against his forehead told the end had come.

As darkness crept in, Buckshot formed his final whispered words with bloody lips. "You are damned, McCreedy." His fading eyes yet reflected ironclad certainty that wickedness could not evade eternal justice, in this world or the next.

McCreedy's reply was the click of the hammer being drawn back. But the gunshot that followed was not his own - the outlaw leader jerked and spilled sideways, a bullet through his brain. Cries of shock and rage erupted from the remaining gang members as they spun about wildly. Had salvation come?

From his paralyzed position sprawled on the floor, Buckshot had no view of whatever miracle had intervened to spare him instant death and slay McCreedy. But strangled voices shouted "The sheriff's here! It's a posse!" along with screams and pleading not to shoot. The sounds of violence quickly ceased, replaced by unfamiliar voices barking questions demanding to know if Buckshot still lived. Hope flickered anew, though his ravaged body seemed beyond salvaging.

Strong hands gently rolled Buckshot over onto his back. Through fading vision he made out the sheriff's face peering down at him, buckskin jacket splattered with blood not his own. The lawman blanched seeing the wounds, yelling desperately for the doctor to hurry. "Stay with us, Buck! Hang on now, y'hear?"

But the light was disappearing rapidly, drawing Buckshot away to whatever lay beyond. He felt only profound relief that McCreedy had been stopped and Deadwood saved, even at such cost. His spirit was ready as beckoning darkness enfolded him. Each shallow breath crept closer to the last. The guns at last fell silent. With a final whispered goodbye to his precious Violet, Buckshot Roberts passed gently into legend, his task complete.

In the days that followed, grief hung heavy over Deadwood like stormclouds refusing to break. The sheriff and townsmen carried Buckshot's body reverently to the small white-steepled church where he lay in state beneath a multiplicity of flowers and candles. Even former critics came to pay respects to the steadfast savior who had placed himself bodily between innocents and annihilation when no other would.

Violet remained almost constantly at the coffin side, dry-eyed and calm in her sorrow, sometimes speaking softly to Buckshot as though they were not parted. The sheriff stared down uncomfortably at his boots when she thanked him for finally mobilizing the posse, too late though it had proven. Those days waiting helplessly indoors while violence tore the town apart had nearly crushed Violet's spirit. But she bore no grudge against the lawman. What was done could not be undone. They must look forward now.

The day of the funeral dawned sunny and clear, as if the heavens too wished to honor the fallen champion. A long cortege of mourners led by Violet walked slowly behind the humble horse-drawn wagon bearing Buckshot's cherrywood casket to the cemetery outside town. There he was laid to rest beneath the shade of a beautiful silver maple where birds chorused and a marble monument was soon erected.

Violet remained until dusk fell, sitting quietly by the grave as shadows stretched long. Finally she placed a single red rose atop the fresh mound. "Until we are together again in spirit, my love," she whispered through bittersweet tears. Then with head held high, Violet walked away down the lamp-lit lane toward an uncertain future, but one she would face with the same brave spirit that had so inspired her lost love. Though Buckshot was gone, the hope which had flourished with him endured, kindled in the many lives he had impacted for the better. Where love and courage persist, the light can never be wholly extinguished. Thus his memory remained a shining beacon for others who heard tell of his selfless sacrifice, changing hearts and minds long after the man himself passed into myth and folk legend.

Chapter 17 - Billy the Kid Escapes

A storm raged through the night after the bloody confrontation between Buckshot and McCreedy's gang in the streets of Deadwood. Thunder shook the window panes as rain pounded the roof, drowning out the moans of wounded men. By dawn, the deluge had settled into a grey drizzle cloaking the town.

In the muted morning light, grim-faced townsfolk emerged cautiously to survey the battle's aftermath. The main street was a sea of muddy churned earth and debris. Crimson stains told of lives spilled upon the ground. The saloon where Buckshot had made his final stand now slumped a charred ruin. It was a solemn procession that came to carry his broken body from that place once the fires died down.

The drizzle persisted as Buckshot was borne to the small white-steepled church and laid before the altar under vigil candles. Violet kept stoic watch over her fallen beloved, dry-eyed but calm in her sorrow. When the sheriff approached, hat in hand, she extended her own to squeeze his arm. "Regret solves nothing," she whispered. "We must look to the future now." Her grace made the lawman duck his head in shame at doing too little, too late.

The funeral was held when finally the rain relented, though skies remained broodingly overcast. The procession of mourners stretched far out from the church, following the wagon bearing Buckshot's casket to the cemetery where he was laid to rest beneath a spreading silver maple. A lone red rose on his grave from Violet marked farewell rather than end - love transcending loss.

Meanwhile, the remnant of McCreedy's now leaderless gang had scrambled in disarray after the fight, abandoning their dead and wounded comrades. Driven on by fear of the posse, they did not stop that whole day and night, putting many hard miles between themselves and Deadwood. Finally the bedraggled outlaws collapsed in an exhausted, mud-caked heap at a secluded canyon campsite.

As the survivors rested their aching bodies, disbelief and outrage grew regarding McCreedy's death. That invincible devil shot down by the town sheriff's last-minute posse? It seemed impossible. Rancor festered within the gang against letting that lawman get the drop on them. They should have immolated all Deadwood that day, leaving no one left to testify what had transpired.

In the absence of McCreedy's iron will to direct them, chaos reigned in the camp. Paranoia flourished as men accused others of fleeing too soon or being spies against the gang. Fistfights erupted as tensions boiled over. What had been a tight-knit crew now fractured into distrustful factions eyeing each other across sputtering campfires.

Amidst the uncertainty, several of McCreedy's longtime lieutenants vied ferociously to seize leadership over the gang. The victor was a hulking brute named Jed Watkins who had grown up with McCreedy. Lacking cunning, Watkins ruled by fear, promising to continue McCreedy's work extorting settlements across the territory. But he struggled to control the gang's in-dependent-minded survivors. They were held together now only by hatred against Deadwood.

Over the following days the mood shifted from shock into lust for vengeance. The story spread that it was Buckshot alone who had shot down McCreedy before being killed himself. That infamous gunslinger had robbed the gang of their leader and glory. He must be made to pay, even if posthumously. All agreed Deadwood must be punished ruthlessly for harboring the tyrant Buckshot.

When scouts reported the town had let down its guard after the recent violence, the time was ripe for reprisals. Watkins has-tily assembled a raid to plunder and burn Deadwood before the sheriff could muster defenses again. Even those grumbling at his leadership were eager to unleash mayhem after simmering impa-tiently in the dreary canyon camp. Within hours, the reborn gang was thundering south brimming with bitterness and bloodlust. Before Buckshot's corpse was even cold, the wolves were already at Deadwood's door again.

Approaching Deadwood stealthily under moonless skies, Watkins halted the gang at a safe distance to finalize their attack plan. The settlement's continued existence offended them. To-night they would level it street-by-street if need be until nothing remained standing. This defiance could not go unpunished. The air fairly vibrated with shared outrage and conviction amongst the circle of grim faces flickering in firelight - Deadwood must burn.

Dividing into smaller teams, the gang infiltrated the unsuspecting town from all sides. Dwellings were surrounded to block escape routes while watkins and his most trusted men moved in to secure the main street. All was silent but for barking dogs that were quickly silenced. The poor citizens of Deadwood had no inkling of the peril encroaching from the shadows.

At Watkins' signal, the gang converged from the darkness, unleashing pandemonium. Windows shattered as pistols fired wildly into homes. Cries of shock gave way immediately to screams of pain and terror. Men were gunned down attempting to defend their families against the invaders. No mercy was given this night, only swift oblivion.

Over the bedlam Watkins bellowed "Burn it down!" as he tossed whiskey jugs to splash and ignite the wooden structures. In minutes much of the street was engulfed in roaring flames. Holy vengeance against the lowly inhabitants who had defied and killed McCreedy! Let their Sodom of hypocrisy and lies be swept away in purifying fire!

Outlaws galloped whooping through the blazing chaos, firing at anything that moved. The gang's fury was terrible in its release after simmering so long thwarted. At last they were delivering justice while the wretched cowered in their homes fit only as pyres. All these years of sworn allegiance to McCreedy culminated in this glorious reckoning upon the town that murdered him.

From the dark periphery, lone unseen rifles cracked methodically, dropping rampaging gang members from their saddles. Cries of alarm went up - where was this ambush coming from? The trap had become the quarry. As their numbers swiftly dwindled under accurate fire, panic set in, breaking the spell of bloodlust that gripped the gang.

Before Watkins could rally them to stand and fight, his skull erupted in red ruin from the unseen sniper's bullet. Leaderless again and their thinned ranks still taking losses, the gang lost any semblance of order. It became a frantic rout to slip the noose now pulled tight around them as shadowy lawmen charged into the firelit streets with buckshot and bullet whizzing through the smoky air. A town they had expected to find easy prey was now a bastion of death raining relentlessly upon them. Their vengeance had horribly backfired.

As the outlaw survivors scrambled for the outskirts, further disaster struck. Fresh torchlight appeared along with shouted commands to surrender. It was the sheriff with an armed posse flanking their escape path, responding swiftly to the first sounds of trouble. Realizing they were surrounded and doomed, the remnants of the gang threw down their weapons in bitter defeat. After coming so close to exterminating Deadwood, only pitiless irons and hemp awaited them now.

Amidst the chaos and confusion, one shadowy figure slipped unseen between buildings, refusing surrender. Billy recognized impending disaster the instant Watkins fell dead - this bold raid had become a death trap. There was no glory to be won here anymore. While the sheriff and his men rounded up the remaining gang members at gunpoint, Billy reached his horse and stole swiftly into the night.

The next morning revealed a scene of devastation, though the fires had been contained faster than anticipated. Bodies were still being pulled from the smoldering ruins. But Deadwood had rallied and endured somehow. The Sheriff organized work crews to start immediate cleanup while rounding up witnesses to piece together the previous night's violence. Someone had clearly set a cunning trap for the outlaws while evacuating citizens out of harm's way. But who?

As the dazed townspeople emerged to confront the wreckage, there strode into their midst a man they had never expected to see again - a lean figure in buckskins carrying an express rifle, face shrouded beneath a familiar broken-brimmed hat. Unsure murmurs rippled through the crowd. How was this possible? Buckshot Roberts was dead and buried! A ghost come back to haunt them?

The sheriff stepped forward warily, hand poised near his holstered pistol. But then the apparition tipped back his hat, revealing not Buckshot but a similar weathered face with darker eyes and beard. A woman's gasp carried through the stunned silence - Violet! She swayed on her feet, grabbing the sheriff's arm for support. "Cole?" she whispered incredulously.

"Hey there, little sister," Cole Roberts said quietly, embracing her. "We got your telegram just in time." Violet burst into tears as she clutched her brother tight. Buckshot's elder brother had arrived from out East, summoned by Violet once McCreedy's gang had first menaced Deadwood. Receiving no further word, Cole had set up the crafty ambush to be ready whichever way the wind blew. In Buckshot's absence, Cole had become Deadwood's stalwart protector against those who would still do it harm.

His face grim, Cole helped Violet over to sit by the town well. "I'm sorry I didn't reach here sooner," he said heavily. "Maybe James would still be..." Unable to finish, Cole hung his head sorrowfully. Violet lifted his chin until their eyes met. "You're here now when we need you most," she told him firmly. "This town is as much your home to defend now as it ever was James'." Gazing over the ruined street, Cole finally nodded, jaw set. There was indeed much righteous work ahead rebuilding Deadwood.

And so the Roberts brothers became the twin pillars supporting the town through those bleak times. Cole helped organize militia patrols and rallies of solidarity against the last remnants of McCreedy's still marauding gang. Meanwhile Violet rebuilt her beloved schoolhouse that had burned, teaching with patience and compassion to help heal young souls affected by the violence. She kept candles lit at Buckshot's grave through many seasons, never forgetting the man who had turned from darkness to become Deadwood's champion.

The rest of Billy's scattered gang soon heard of the disastrous raid on Deadwood, along with their many compatriots now awaiting hangman's justice. They turned on Billy savagely, accusing him of masterminding the debacle that left them ruined and disgraced. But Billy pleaded ignorance, swearing all had seemed in their favor when he withdrew, leaving leadership to the foolish Watkins.

brandeHowever the verdict fell, their now meager crew had no stomach left for confronting Deadwood and its defenders again. The gang swiftly fell apart amidst angry recriminations. Some headed south planning to resume plundering the lawless tracks into Mexico that McCreedy had first rode up years ago. Others simply wandered off to find lone fates among the endless wide-open frontier. Their saga of brotherhood-in-arms had ended bitterly.

Billy rode the high passes for long months alone, refusing to admit defeat. If he could not have the immortality he craved through legend, he would embrace the other kind - that of the rogue wolf too cunning for traps or bullets to end his marauding freedom. All the petty rules of sheep and shepherds were not for him. As snow blanketed the high country, driving weaker creatures down, Billy felt only contempt. They would never know what it meant to live fierce and unfettered.

When at last even he was forced lower amidst spring thaw, Billy eluded lonely death through his unmatched mastery of the wilderness. Ravenous predators shied from his camp, unwilling to risk the madness revealed in his hollow eyes. The mountains, once haven and playground, had become only bitter mockery of that irrecoverable brotherhood now dissolved through fate and folly. Isolated freedom was purer punishment. For redemption, Billy rode once more toward human company on the frontier fringe. There perhaps some new pack would allow him in, knowing not the shadows he bore. Until then, only the wild called tryly without recrimination or regret. That alone must sustain him one more season. Wherever the wind blew, no anchor held Billy any longer.

Chapter 18 - The Town Buries a Hero

A heavy pall hung over Deadwood the morning after Buckshot Roberts finally met his destiny in the street. Throughout the ravaged town, survivors stumbled about numbly, consoling loved ones or surveying the damage done during the ferocious battle against McCreedy's now vanquished gang.

The saloon where Buckshot had made his valiant last stand was a roofless ruin, charred and bullet-ridden. With heads bowed solemnly, the sheriff and some townsmen entered to retrieve what they could of their fallen hero. They found Buckshot's body crumpled behind the bar riddled with slugs, his skin cold to the touch. But there was no mistaking the defiant glint still frozen in his open eyes. He had faced the end unbowed, defiant to the finish.

With infinite care, they lifted their savior's broken form and made a procession towards the small white-steepled chapel on the hill that had so often given Buckshot solace from worldly troubles. There they reverently laid him upon the humble altar and draped a flag over the casket. The preacher himself knelt to offer last rites beseeching the Lord's mercy upon this flawed but noble soul. By sundown, candles encircled the bier flickering warmly as if welcoming Buckshot home.

Outside, townsfolk kept mournful vigil throughout the night, filling the air with hymns of sorrow and hope. The sheriff stood sentry beside the casket, hat pressed over his heart, refusing to abandon Buckshot even now at the final hour. He silently berated himself again for not mustering the posse sooner. But dwelling on past failings served nothing. Their guardian was gone and Deadwood forever changed. All they could do was bid him farewell with the honor he deserved.

As grey dawn seeped through the stained glass windows, a lone woman entered the hushed chapel and made her way between the votives towards the flag-draped coffin. Violet, Buckshot's beloved, walked as one enchanted, never taking her eyes from his silhouette beneath the shroud. Only the slight quaver of her hands betrayed the depth of anguish she carried silently. Reaching Buckshot's side at last, she leaned down to rest her head upon his chest as if listening for the missing heartbeat. Dry-eyed, she murmured tenderly to him too softly for any others to hear.

The sun rose higher in the sky, coaxing activity from the town outside as a new day daunted them, empty without their champion. One by one, more citizens filtered into the chapel to pay respects beneath Buckshot's resting place. Some spoke a few words of praise, others just shook their heads sorrowfully. Many left tokens - cards, flowers, a lucky horseshoe. The small altar slowly disappeared beneath these humble gifts.

Often someone would gently ask Violet if she needed rest or nourishment. But she refused to leave her post, wrapped in inconsolable thoughts understandable to her alone. The sheriff finally insisted at least a chair be brought for her vigil. "You're one of the strongest souls I ever saw, Miss Violet," he told her somberly. "We won't trouble you no more. But let us know if there's any way we can ease your burden." Violet silently placed her hand on his weathered one and squeezed once in gratitude. She had no need of comfort except being near her beloved.

Later, passersby were surprised to hear the sound of lively gospel hymns emanating from within the chapel. There they beheld Violet standing before the coffin softly singing Buckshot's favorite sacred melodies. Her clear, sweet voice pulled at their hearts, bringing tears and smiles alike. In that simple act of devotion, Violet lifted the pall of gloom from the sanctuary, letting in hope and balm for all present. Some joined their voices to hers until the old walls echoed with faith and sublime sorrow. Buckshot would have cherished this stirring farewell.

Too soon, the lowering sun's rays streaming through the windows summoned the mournful hour. Six of the burliest men about town took up the coffin and walked it slowly outside followed by the procession of honoring mourners. The wagon that would bear Buckshot to his final rest awaited, festooned with garlands by caring hands. But before they loaded him aboard, the small crowd hushed in expectation. The little preacher stepped forth into the lantern light.

Clearing his throat, the preacher searched for eloquence equal to his subject but found none. "I will let the great Bard speak for us in this solemn hour," he explained, opening a leatherbound book. There upon the twilit street, he read aloud Shakespeare's passage on Marc Antony's funeral oration:

"His life was gentle, and the elements So mix'd in him that Nature might stand up And say to all the world, 'This was a man!'"

A profound silence followed when he finished. Rugged faces surrounding shone with tears in the flicker of sconces. The preacher reverently closed his book. "Go with God, Buckshot Roberts," he intoned softly. "May flights of angels sing thee to thy rest, thou noble spirit."

With that benediction given, the pallbearers finally loaded Buckshot's casket respectfully unto the wagon before climbing aboard themselves. Violet was assisted up to sit beside the driver. As the solemn procession left behind the chapel and weary town, neighbors lined the route holding lanterns in silent tribute. From the gloom, strains of gentle Amazing Grace trailed after the swaying funerary lamp lights as they dwindled into the prairie night.

After a mile, the wagon halted at the small fenced graveyard overlooking Deadwood in the valley below. There beside the swaying silver maples, a freshly dug grave lay waiting to reunite Buckshot with the sanctified earth. While crickets chirped softly, his casket was lifted down and borne to the brink of eternity. Violet pressed her forehead tenderly against the lacquered wood one final time. "Farewell, my love," she whispered through quivering lips. "You light the way home for me."

The humble service completed as the last clods scattered atop the mound, the mourners began their weary walk back to town, leaving Violet by the grave. Finally alone with her grief beneath the glittering stars, she let flow the sorrow beyond tears as her heart broke. She bent as if physically pummeled by loss's cruel blow. But there was also gratitude - for this man who had blessed her life beyond deserving; for the town which survived through his sacrifice. She had been left bereft, but not alone. Love remained that conquered even darkest night.

Drawing her shawl close against the prairie chill, Violet walked the lonesome road through moonlight back to Deadwood. She moved now with head erect, heart certain that none truly died who lived on in others. Her steps followed the light Buckshot's valiant soul still kindled to guide all who walked in darkness towards grace. She would mourn hard, but not forever. Buckshot was now part of this land he had defended. And she would continue the good work, one foot steadfastly before the other until they met again in a place beyond tears or farewells. For in her he would always live on.

The next week saw Deadwood slowly recover its shaken spirit as citizens joined together to begin mending all that had been rent asunder. The day Buckshot was laid to rest became a milestone - the darkness had lifted. He had given his life so they could continue building something good here. The town must prove itself worthy of his gift.

Anecdotes and fond remembrances were shared of the brave gunslinger who drove off predators and helped honest folk without reward. While time might blur memories, these stories would be passed down so Deadwood always remembered the broken man who found redemption in defending others. A rough-hewn granite monument was soon erected over his grave with a carved marble plaque reading simply:

BUCKSHOT Roberts Our Champion & Avenger No Greater Love Hath A Man Than To Lay Down His Life For His Friends

Beneath the inscription was engraved an open book, symbol of Buckshot's hard-won wisdom, with his Colt pistols crossed behind - reminders of a storied past never fully forgotten. He was now part of this community's living history. All drifters eventually find home.

Chapter 19 - The Legend Lives On

In the weeks following Buckshot Roberts's funeral, life in Deadwood gradually regained a semblance of normalcy as the hardy citizens focused their energy on rebuilding all that had been destroyed by McCreedy's marauders.

Boarding up shattered windows, repairing bullet holes, and sweeping away debris kept bodies occupied during daylight hours. At sunset, the ringing of hammers was replaced by solemn hymns floating on the evening air as families gave thanks for being spared from the full measure of chaos narrowly averted.

Hardship brought the township closer together, tightening bonds between disparate souls now wedded by adversity.

Nights often found the people congregated around crackling bonfires on the main street in solidarity and celebration of endurance. There they sang songs, told tales, and shared meager victuals like long-parted pilgrims reunited. The names of those lost were spoken aloud to hallow their memory. And always the story was retold of one flawed but valiant gunslinger who helped salvage their community against impossible odds when all seemed lost. Already the moments were passing into legend.

Out on the prairie's edge, lit by flickering fireflies beneath the wheeling heavens, Violet kept her own counsel over a humble mound littered with modest arrangements and hand-drawn cards bearing children's halting condolences. There she sat late into the darkness, shawl wrapped tightly round her slender frame as wind-teased grass whispered all around. Whatever inner dialogue passed in those far hours between heart and heavens remained hers alone, unbreachable by comforters. But Violet's inherent spirit kept her steady on course when the sun rose again. She understood well there were others who still needed her compass bearing while charting their own passage through less navigable straits. This purpose braced her steps against faltering during the light's cruel hours.

Recognizing Violet's quiet perseverance, the townswomen soon joined together in an effort to construct a proper headstone and monument commemorating their fallen hero. While survivor menfolk focused on practical rebuilding tasks, this women's brigade collected spare stones and bricks, mixing adobe mortar and shaping it over a wooden form. Their children scavenged in creek beds for colorful smooth rocks to stud across the gray façade. At midday, the industrious crew sang hymns together to raise blistered spirits, holding fast to their vision. in their imaginations, Violet's sad yearly pilgrimage to a weedy plot was transmuted into a radiant beacon honoring virtue's strugglerequired of all humankind, ever imperfect but improving.

When the modest but noble memorial edifice finally took shape and hardened after weeks of baking in the prairie's endless summer sun, preparations immediately began for an unveiling ceremony on the anniversary of that fateful day Buckshot sacrificed himself defending innocents. Handbills went up, a children's choir was organized, and townspeople spent evenings pressing their few good garments by candlelight in anticipation. For this solemn occasion celebrating courage's triumph over evil's maw, the sensibilities of the urbane East were adapted to rustic frontier surroundings as best prairie folk knew how. Their roughhewn sincerity had to substitute for high refinement in rendering respects.

On the chosen evening, what seemed the entire population of Deadwood turned out for the dedication event and solemn pilgrimage to the remote burial ground where their protector rested eternally. Led by the sheriff hoisting a tattered Stars and Stripes snatched as spoils from McCreedy's routed mob, the impromptu procession marched two by two behind buckboard wagons bearing the shrouded monument and stonemason's tools required for installation. Spectral dust plumes marked the righteous convoy's passage across the wide prairie beneath a fiery orange sunset. Parents lifted small children onto shoulders so they might forever retell this twilight journey paying homage to

Old West heroes of peerless mettle. Who could say what seeds of courage and resilience were sown in those young hearts during their reverent march over the endless grasslands?

Reaching the cemetery plots as Venus peeked between veils of purple dusk, lamps were lit and the wagons carefully off-loaded by the small gaggle of stonecutters tasked as honor guard. As a setting half-moon slowly crested the horizon, townspeople fanned out lighting candles both to illuminate labors and lend atmosphere befitting the moment. A cappella voices rehearsed their musical tribute softly as block and tackle were assembled and horse teams harnessed to erect the monument. By lantern light, the component stones were quietly mortared in place atop Buckshot's ring of stones - a five-foot obelisk carved front and back with soaring eagles and crashing ocean waves. This lithic metaphor evoked the indomitable frontier spirit. Bordering the monolith's base, embedded river stones spelled out the inscription "Our Defender" in deliberately rough-hewn relief. Form and text alike exuded eternal solidity. Once satisfied the monument stood centered plum and square, the masons packed their tools and joined the murmuring onlookers already reverently circling the memorial. Clearing his throat nervously, the mayor stepped forward holding crumpled pages with words he had labored weeks composing in spare moments. At his cue, the children's choir piped up sweetly with a rendition of Rock of Ages suitable to the setting. Then the mayor began reading by lamplight his elaborate speech extolling virtues, recounting highlights of Buckshot's valiant stand, and portending this beacon would shine moral encouragement over future generations. Those gathered nodded and dabbed tears at poignant junctures.

When the mayor concluded his wordy remarks, an expectant pause followed, as if the monument itself might voice acknowledgment of their esteem. But only the restless stamping of draft horses and subdued sobs from the youthful choir disturbed the twilight air. Gradually group attention shifted back to the mayor, who flushed self-consciously realizing no miraculous response was forthcoming. Clearing his throat again awkwardly, he raised his hand in habitual benediction.

But before the gesture was completed, Violet emerged silently from the onlookers' shadows where she had listened pensively. All stirred as she approached alone to stand before the stark granite pillar now guarding her innermost heart's treasure. Reaching out, her fingers slowly traced the deeply-carved letters spelling her late husband's enduring pseudonym. Eyes closed, Violet seemed to commune with the stone spiritils of righteous sacrifice and unvanquished hope enshrined there.

After several moments of mystical connection, Violet withdrew an object cradled in both hands and bent to nestle it at the monument's base where grey rock met fertile earth. When she straightened again, twin tears streaked her delicate cheeks in the lambent glow. But her purposeful expression remained tranquil.

Stepping back, Violet lifted her gaze to openly address the assembled citizens. "My friends," she began quietly but clearly, "let this likeness in unfeeling mineral ever remind us that it was flesh and blood courage which stood fast when evil loomed, demanding similar bravery in us. Though taken from this world prematurely, our steadfast guardian's example shall persist, enlivening generations yet unborn. Death's veil cannot dim the illumination of valor shared selflessly even once amongst us."

She paused, looking each listener in the eyes. "This light guides our way forward through fear and doubt. Here stands symbol, not deity. James Roberts rests now only in the land and Lord's keeping. His mission on earth was completed with honor. Ours continues by the light he helped ignite. We memorialize him best by fanning that flickering flame within our own hearts. For light reveals life's pathway, but only if we bear it forward undimmed."

Tears shone in more eyes than Violet's now as she concluded softly, "Let us fulfill James's legacy by living as he died - standing resolute with head held high when shadows threaten. That is the flame he lit, the torch we must bear bravely onward." With these final words, Violet nodded graciously to the mayor then turned away into lantern shadows surrounding. For his part, the mayor could barely murmur "amen" through the lump in his throat before likewise hastily retreating from the weight of emotions loosed.

In hushed clusters, the rest of those gathered dabbed wet cheeks and exchanged embraces, processing Violet's extemporized but heart-piercing exhortation. By unspoken assent, candles were finally extinguished, tools gathered, and animals harnessed to depart the graveside without further remarks. Much inner contemplation would continue in isolated homesteads long after the closing hymn's final strains faded over the darkened prairie.

As wagons slowly rolled past towards distant twinkling campfires marking Deadwood, not a soul glanced back to mark Violet's black silhouette remaining motionless beside the towering obelisk, one slender hand resting on rough granite. There let her keep solitary communion under nebulae wheeling slowly overhead. What more needed now be said or done? Sometimes less is more. In the humble work of blessing dedications and raising memorials, the living gained surprising closure unhoped for. Let Violet gather herself in the silent hours. Dawn would arrive soon enough, demanding her attention anew. Tonight belonged to the bereaved and their visions by moonlight. For who can know all the powers stirred by faithful remembrance bound to earthly good?

www.ingramcontent.com/pod-product-compliance
Lightning Source LLC
Chambersburg PA
CBHW071326130726
47996CB00002B/645